A
HARLEQUIN
Book

1348

REVOLT — AND VIRGINIA

by

ESSIE SUMMERS

HARLEQUIN BOOKS

WINNIPEG ● CANADA

First published in 1969 by Mills & Boon Limited,
50 Grafton Way, Fitzroy Square, London, England.

SBN 373-01348-5

© Essie Summers 1969

Harlequin Canadian edition published November, 1969
Harlequin U.S. edition published February, 1970

To

Dorothy Steere, of Eastbourne

in admiration

*All the characters in this book have no existence outside the
imagination of the Author, and have no relation whatsoever to
anyone bearing the same name or names. They are not even
distantly inspired by any individual known or unknown to the
Author, and all the incidents are pure invention.*

Printed in Canada

To

Dorothy Steere, of Eastbourne
in admiration

The common problem, yours and mine,
Is not to fancy what were fair in life
Provided it could be; but finding first
What may be, then find how to make it fair
Up to our means ... a very different thing.
— *Robert Browning*

CHAPTER ONE

AFTERWARDS Virginia was sure the new hair-do had triggered off the whole train of events. Because she had been endowed with thick, shining red hair that fell naturally into modern sweeping smoothness, she rarely bothered with professional shampoos and sets, but last night she had been visiting Anne Redway's flat and had been persuaded into this ultra-sophisticated style.

Anne worked at the beauty salon at Warrington's where Virginia was advertising clerk, and she had a sun-porch rigged up as a miniature salon at her flat and was always persuading some trusting friend to act as guinea-pig for a new creation she wanted to try out on paying clients in the near future.

Mother had been enraptured with it when she beheld it the next morning and her comments had caused Father to emerge from behind his newspaper and view it with horror, vocally expressed a moment later.

Mother had giggled. 'Take no notice of him, Virginia. Men just hate their women to change their hairstyles.'

Father had looked outraged. 'We do not. But the other way suited her better. It was sweet and girlish.'

Virginia and her mother had exchanged glances. Virginia said: 'Darling Dad, don't you remember when I first had it that way . . . you thought it was hard and plain? You preferred me with long, dangling tresses. Trouble is, darling, I've spoiled you. Most girls change their styles every second week. I'm always too much interested in other things besides hair to do that, so you can't stand me in any other style.'

'Nothing of the kind,' he had muttered, 'it's simply a case of knowing what I like,' and retired with a snort to a prolonged study of the weather map.

But the hair-do had certainly had an effect on Les Warrington. Virginia had always been friendly with him, but as a rule his taste in girls ran to something more flamboyant.

True, he had once said to her, 'You've got the looks – why did you have to be a bookworm?' but in the main their relationship had been purely one of business.

When he came into Virginia's office, Madge Merton, the office junior, was bending over a table cutting out Warrington's advertisements and pasting them in a huge scrapbook. Adela Murray was measuring them with a ruler and copying the results into a ledger, prior to passing them for payment. Virginia was at her typewriter, fingers flying.

'Sorry to interrupt the good work, girls,' said Les in his usual pleasant fashion, 'but I'd like you to go along the street to Smyrnington's and unobtrusively take notes of the wording and prices of their new autumn showcases. Not frocks and millinery, but the accessories. I suppose you can spare them, Miss Fergusson?'

Virginia nodded. 'Yes, they're well up to date with that. They're on this morning's paper now. They've finished the weeklies.'

The girls disappeared and Les stayed chatting. 'I'd like to get on with those details for the pictorials this afternoon and the magazine advertisements. Get out your pad and we'll rough them out.'

Virginia moved to a pile of magazines on a cupboard. 'These American magazines came in this morning and there are some super advertisements in them, extremely novel.'

'Oh, good. Right.' He looked about him. There was a section of glass panelling half way up the wall between this one and the next office. He said, critically, 'This light is too strong, I think. Besides, it bothers me to have that bunch of gigglers watching me all the time. They seem to regard a boss as a sort of rare zoological specimen.' He pulled down the blinds.

Virginia said: 'I didn't think the light was as strong as all that at the moment. I think that's a bit dark. Shall I pull them up just a little?'

'No, decidedly not. They'll peep underneath. Distracts us – and them. Sit over here, Virginia, we'll get the light from that skylight then. One of these days I'll have that glass removed and the whole thing filled in with some light panelling. I was suggesting it to my mother just last weekend.'

He indicated a long form in front of the desk that held newspaper files. The two other girls often worked here.

They got busy on the magazines, Virginia taking down notes in shorthand as they worked them out.

The rest of the shop seemed pleasingly distant, the incessant clacketty-clack of the typewriters in the adjoining office – shutting them off from the coming and going of customers and the whirr of lifts and escalators.

A girl from the cafeteria brought them their afternoon tea. Les had a cigarette and they settled to work again. They finished a new and different idea of advertising haberdashery lines and started on the lingerie department.

Virginia reached out for the American magazines. 'They've been very lavish here,' she said. There was a full-page illustration that must have cost the earth. The background was glossy blue. The caption read: 'Atlantic Honeymoon ...' and the picture was of part of the deck of an enormous liner silhouetted against a velvety sky complete with stars and moon, and showing two shadowy figures almost merged into one. On the opposite page was a glimpse of a cabin in the bridal suite with all sorts of dainty negligées frothing out of a super de luxe travelling case. Beneath this was the inevitable list of prices.

Les Warrington looked interested but doubtful. 'Don't think we've got much scope for that in little old New Zealand,' he said.

Virginia's eyes, brilliantly green beneath the copper brows, flashed with indignation. She said scornfully, 'It's just the same in the advertising world as in the literary world! Nobody puts any glamour round New Zealand, therefore it's *got* no glamour as far as overseas is concerned! People simply expect New Zealand books to be written

9

about sheep and mountains, lakes and plains! Nobody ever uses the background of university life here in Dunedin, or pictures it as a Southern Hemisphere Oxford – what about our Medical School and the instances of its products winning fame overseas? What about the tropical beauty of Auckland – the mixture of sea-port and Capital flavour of Wellington – the night life of our cities—'

Les Warrington stared, then laughed: 'What do you know about night life?'

Virginia swept on: 'And it's just the same in advertising. It's far too stodgy, far too conservative to try new ideas. It gives me no scope for imagination at all. It's positively galling ... cramping. No wonder advertising clerks with any go in them go off to Australia or England ... there's never any imagery in *our* advertising. If you get an advertising clerk with a few ideas – what happens? The heads of the firm mutter unhappily that it's never been done before and think wistfully of the days when they could advertise ladies' wool and cotton vests, short sleeves, shaped waists; or natural coloured winter-weight combinations, fully-gusseted, double-seamed, wearing qualities guaranteed and every garment shrink-proof!'

She stopped for breath and Les Warrington blinked. 'Here! Am I being called a stuffed shirt? Am I one of these conservative heads? What a nerve! Let me tell you, my girl, combinations had gone out before I was born, much less started in the firm! Come on, redhead, get it off your chest ... what kind of ads would you like to see us splash out on?'

Virginia rummaged in a pile of newspapers, found what she wanted and pointed triumphantly to a travel agency's advertisement. 'See, "Island cruises ... these cruises last three weeks ... Fiji, Samoa, Tonga, glamorous French-speaking New Caledonia, Raratonga ... all the romantic and fabulous atmosphere of the Pacific ... coral reefs, still lagoons, coconut palms ... book now for March and April." '

She looked at her boss. 'We could make capital out of

that. We could work in with the agencies and have a blitz on the travelling public. You know ... really splash, Mr. Warrington. Have a heading – a really outsize one: "Why be so stuffy about your holidays?" and follow up with ... um ... "Why only read about other people taking fabulous cruises? They're within your reach and your financial means ... and all within the confines of your three-week vacation from business." Then go to town on what they'll need: Say, "Pacific Cruise ... star-dusted nights, languorous moons, sapphire seas, white beaches, shadowy palms ... and you can take glamour with you too ... in that suitcase you'll buy, of course, at Warrington's travel department. Visit our lingerie section, buy exotic garments, all laciness and colour, fit for a princess or a film star, yet yours for an incredibly reasonable outlay ... to suit a workaday girl's purse ... a girl with dreams in her eyes ...'

She stopped, because Les Warrington was chuckling at her eagerness.

He looked at her with eyes that were appreciative of her enthusiasm, 'You've got something there. No wonder they reckon the wording of our adverts is the best in the South Island!'

Virginia flushed with pleasure, and her green eyes sparkled.

'Thanks, Mr. Warrington.' She hesitated, then plunged ... 'Listen, I've not told anyone yet, bar Mother and Father – I felt I wanted to keep it to myself for a week or two first, but – well, you know I write a fair bit of fiction in my spare time?'

He nodded. 'Yes, of course. Your short stories and poems and things? I often see them in the magazines when I'm leafing through for ads.'

Virginia said, with shining eyes, 'Well, last week I realized my dearest dream. I got word that the book – a novel – I sent to England just before Christmas has been accepted.'

He grasped her hand. 'You've done well, at your age. Congratulations! We'll bask in your reflected glory. Even the shop will take on an added lustre in everyone's eyes.

When are you going to tell the papers? Would you like me to do that for you? But I've just thought. It won't mean you'll leave the firm and devote yourself to writing, will it?

Virginia laughed. 'Oh, Les! – I mean Mr. Warrington! One book doesn't make an author! I've far to go before I can do that.'

'Just as well for us – we don't want to lose you.'

They chatted on for a few moments about her success, and Virginia quite appreciated his interest because she knew full well that this was sheer kindness on his part as he was, as far as literature went, a sheer Philistine, even if a shrewd young business man.

She wasn't to know Les was enjoying this somewhat new Virginia, watching the colour come and go in the vivid face so close to his as they sat on the form.

She was suddenly aware that she was talking far too much about herself, her hopes and aspirations, so she said crisply:

'Well, I suppose we'd better return to our ads. This isn't what you pay me for! What about getting Mr. McKinlay in to do some rough sketches?' She reached out a hand to pick up the house telephone.

Les's hand closed over her wrist and drew her back. 'Don't bother for a moment. I have other ideas.' A flash of mischief lit his merry dark eyes, his arm went round her shoulder, and he drew her against him.

Virginia was taken completely by surprise. His eyes laughed down into hers. 'You're very sweet, you know, and – rather full of surprises today.' And he kissed her full on the lips, even as she stiffened in protest.

They heard the door open. Virginia pushed Les aside in real panic. If any of those scatty girls next door saw this, it would be all over the store by closing-time!

She looked straight up into his mother's furious face! And wished it had belonged to one of the scatty girls.

Les saw her aghast look and swung round. He swallowed, but couldn't forbear a grin as he got off the form.

'So!' said Martha Warrington. 'No wonder I was looking all over the shop for you! I won't have you making love
to the girls in the shop! I simply *won't* have it!'

Les laughed, and at the sound of that laugh, Virginia,
by reason of all the years she had known him, felt a deep
foreboding. There were times when the divil himself got
into the son of the firm, and he could be outrageous. He
laughed again and said, in a tone of mild objection, 'I'm
not making love to 'em all ... only to Virginia. Besides,
Mother, just as a point of interest, how would you stop
me?'

Martha, for some reason, had never been particularly fond
of Virginia. Martha was extremely temperamental and enjoyed a good fight now and then. She held nothing aginst
any member of the staff who fired up in self-defence, but
she'd always felt Virginia had disdained to reply in kind,
and consequently this sort of cool control had sometimes
infuriated Mrs. Warrington. But she appreciated Virginia's
skill with words and flair for advertising.

But now she forgot how valuable Virginia was to her. 'I
suppose you think,' she said venomously, 'that he'd be a
good match for you ... that he's the sole heir to the business. I've not got him to this age to let him fall for any
girl who sees him as a darned good catch. Let me tell
you, if he doesn't marry to please me, I don't have to leave
him a penny ... and won't!'

Virginia couldn't believe her ears. She had the quick
temper common to most redheads and had got herself into
some rare pickles through losing it, in her teens, but she
had certain good reasons, when she first came to Warrington's, that made it imperative she should retain her well-
paid position. She had taken quite a lot from Martha before
she reached her present standard of work that made her a
valued, not easily replaced, member of the staff.

Now she felt white-hot, though outwardly cool. 'It doesn't
make any difference to me whether you leave him the lot
or none,' she said clearly. 'I'm not in the least interested in
your Leslie *or* his money—' She lifted her chin. 'Imagine

13

me marrying a man who wouldn't know the difference between Rupert Brooke and Ella Wheeler Wilcox or between—'

'That's a dirty slam, if ever there was one,' said Les, who was obviously enjoying the whole thing. He was so used to his mother's tirades; part and parcel of the forceful character that had made Warrington's what it was, but it was most surprising to see the little Fergusson so het-up. And a daughter of the Manse at that! If she really let herself go, she'd be something.

He chipped in again before they had time to do any more than glare at him, 'But I have lots of virtues you'd never suspect, Virginia, and accomplishments, too. I'm a wizard with speed-boats, I may even become famous yet, when I get away from mama's apron-strings ... I'm invariably pleasant at breakfast, and I almost never bite my nails!'

The two women turned back towards each other, completely ignoring him.

'And,' continued Virginia in a cutting tone, as if he had never spoken, 'I'm on the point of announcing my engagement to someone else!'

'Who?' asked Les, with a great show of interest. 'Or are you just trotting that out to put my mother off the scent and to sound dramatic?'

Virginia stopped being white-hot and cool and became red-hot and furious. Her eyes positively blazed. 'Put her off the scent? Have you gone stark, staring mad, Mr. Warrington? You know perfectly well that you've never made a pass at me in your life till now and you took me unawares ... and it's perfectly true, I *am* on the point of becoming engaged ... is there any reason why I shouldn't?'

'No, darling. The only wonder is that you've not been snapped up long ago. Except that you've been a bit stodgy ... not half come-hitherish enough!'

Les was impossible, Virginia decided. It would only aggravate his mother more, and anyway, once she got a bee into her bonnet, nothing on earth would entice it out. Suddenly she lost all her high colour. She turned to where her grey coat hung on a peg. 'Well, it doesn't matter. You're both quite quite mad. I'll just go.'

'Go?' Martha Warrington's temper evaporated as rapidly as it had risen. In another moment, thought Virginia, remembering other fights Martha had had with other staff members, she'll be offering me a rise, or giving me a present!

Martha gulped. 'You don't mean it ... you can't ... nobody walks out of jobs these days. You—'

Virginia managed to smile thinly. 'Don't they? Then perhaps I'm setting a precedent. Because I'm very surely walking out of this one, right now!'

Martha suddenly realized this was serious. She stammered. 'I – oh, you can't – you can't do this to me. There's that sale coming up in ten days' time. I – you – I'll apologize – I—'

'It's not *my* sale,' said Virginia shrewdly, 'and I'm rather tired of the constant rows that have gone on lately. I know business hasn't been so good, and we've all made allowances – though it's been good enough – haven't I crossed my t's and dotted my i's enough? I'm giving you a minute's notice now.'

She pulled open the top drawer of her desk and drew out her handbag and opening it, brought out her pay envelope, intact. She had drawn it only an hour before. She threw it on to a filing cabinet. 'That's a week's salary in lieu of notice!'

She pulled her coat around her, fastened the one button with a hand that did not tremble and said coolly, 'Goodbye.'

Les Warrington lost his nonchalance and reached the door before she did. He took hold of her wrists and held her. 'Virginia, the fault was mine – entirely mine – and I won't let you do this. I took you completely by surprise and you aren't going to suffer for it. Mother can run the shop, but by jove, she can't run *me*. This nonsense about protecting me from the shop-girls has got to stop. It's positively archaic.' He jerked his head at his mother. 'Mother, scram! I can handle this.'

Martha looked at him, delighted surprise in her eyes. Like most masterful women she appreciated masterfulness in a man. Who'd have thought the boy had it in him? She knew she had shamelessly spoiled him as a child, but lately he had shown this hint of steel on one or two occasions. Nevertheless, she wouldn't have expected a direct command like this. At one time he would have resorted to wheedling.

The corners of her still-handsome mouth twitched. Perhaps he had more of his father in him than she had suspected. . . .

Virginia stood by her desk, her face white and stormy. Les put his hands on her shoulders, swung her round to face him.

'Listen, Virginia. Mother has precipitated things. I wasn't just fooling when I kissed you. It was to be only a preliminary. I'm in love with you, Virginia.'

She went to look up impatiently, but the moment she caught his eyes, she laughed. 'Oh, Les, Les! How reckless can you get? You'll get another good advertising clerk without going to lengths like this! You're always in love with someone or other! A born flirt! This is such an opportunity for a dramatic gesture and you can't resist such things. It wouldn't be any use. If you meant it, it would only complicate my job here. And if I stay on, it will be very awkward working with your mother after all I've said. Besides, I'd like a change. I've never done anything else but this, and it wasn't even what I wanted to do in the first place, though I grew to love it. I'm serious about leaving.'

Les pulled her down on to the form, and exerted all his charm – his not inconsiderable charm – to make her change her mind. He managed to kiss her again during this, which pleased him mightily, even if Virginia only laughed at him. But it did not help his cause.

Finally she said to him with a gesture that showed she was weary of the discussion, 'Go away for a quarter of an hour, Les, and I'll think it out.'

Les got up, well pleased, sure the day was almost won.

CHAPTER TWO

VIRGINIA sat still for exactly two minutes after he had gone, just long enough to hear the outer office door closing behind him, then an impish smile touched her lips.

She picked up the scribbling pad which bore the effusion about the ninon nylon lingerie and wrote: 'I *have* thought it out, Les, and have gone. I'm sure I need a change. This is the tide to be taken at the flood and all that. Thanks for the gallant gesture ... though it's not a technique I'd recommend you to use often. Someone might take you seriously and snap you up. Still, who knows? I may use it as a plot for my next novel. Warmest regards, because most of the time I have enjoyed working for you – V. J. Fergusson.'

She thrust it into an envelope, scrawled 'Mr. L. Warrington' on it with a huge blue pencil, and propped it up against a miniature bust that Mr. McKinlay had been using to sketch foundation garments. Then she picked up bag and gloves and let herself out of another door that gave access on to the packing-floor and made her way into Filleul Street.

She hesitated at the corner. Now what? Go home and tell all? No. She had an idea that if she did she would burst into floods of tears. Temper had carried her on till now. But she was starting to feel weepy and it would humiliate her if she dissolved into tears. Besides, Mother and Father had quite enough of parishioners' troubles on their shoulders, without taking on another! And what was it they always said? Action helped. Especially physically.

A bus rumbled to a stop as she reached George Street. The destination sign said Opoho. Yes, a good high hill to climb – that was what she wanted.

Past Woodhaugh Gardens, over the Water of Leith,

then up the hill above the red mellowness of Knox College to the terminus up Signal Hill Road. Even now that new houses climbed the hill above the valley, she was soon right out in the country, climbing steadily towards Centennial Lookout, built there in 1940 to commemorate one hundred years of Colonial history in New Zealand.

The breeze off the tussocks stirred the hair at her temples – Virginia didn't care if it did disturb that hair-style. Look where the darned thing had got her! She kicked a stone out of her way and felt better. She came to the summit, then took the steps down to the lookout, noticing, as always, the piece of rock hewn from that on which Edinburgh Castle stands, and looked out over the dreaming harbour, the open sea beyond, and the city of Dunedin, bright-roofed and sunny, climbing its seven hills and more. How she loved it! Yet one couldn't always stay in one beloved spot!

After she had gazed her fill she climbed a little more and found an outcrop of rock and perched there, her gaze this time more an inward one. Solitude was what she had needed ... at times you just had to get away and think things out for yourself unhindered by other loyalties and opinions. Most of all, the opinions.

Although her anger had evaporated, she still thought of all the scathing things she might have said to Martha Warrington. And when she was through with that satisfying reflection, she started to wonder how she would have handled the situation with Les had his mother not appeared. Probably she'd have dismissed it as lightly as it deserved. Les's nonsense about being serious was just a gesture he had found irresistible, sparked off by his mother's opposition and his own irrepressible love of teasing and high spirits.

Virginia's sense of humour came to her rescue and she laughed aloud. Really, had Martha been Les's wife instead of his mother she couldn't have been more furious!

All of a sudden she wanted Leicester, wanted him to lean her head against, to hear him say, 'Well, what matter, darling? It doesn't matter twopence ... just a few months

18

and we'll get married. Take a temporary job till then! You know I love you, you must.' Better still to hear him say: 'Let's get married as soon as we can ... how about next month?'

Not that she'd ever known Leicester act quite as impulsively as that – but given the right circumstances – which in this case would mean being quite alone with her, and without the dampening influence of *his* mother, he probably would.

Otherwise, things were ideal. Leicester belonged to her own safe little world, one far removed from the competitive, hectic world of drapery. The world she had always known in her own home ... because Leicester's parish was nearly a hundred miles away, tucked into the delightful foothills sou'west of Oamaru, right under the shadows of the Kakanui Mountains.

It was peaceful and wealthy and unspoiled and reminded Virginia of the parish her father had had near Wanganui when she was a small child. She had often known nostalgia for it.

Perhaps she would ring Leicester tonight and tell him of her stormy afternoon. All of a sudden a disloyal thought struck her. How *would* he react? It would be quite too horrible if he thought she ought to have handled it less dramatically. And she had a faint, disquieting suspicion she ought to have done so! Oh, damn. There, even ministers' daughters damned things occasionally.

She looked at her watch. Well, by now she had certainly cooled off and she thought she would carry on her evening's programme exactly as arranged. By the time she walked to the terminus and caught the bus into town it would be about closing-time, and she could get the bus she usually got to Leicester's widowed mother's home a couple of miles from the Bay Manse. Mrs. Gordon need not know – yet – that she had left Warrington's. Time enough for that when Virginia had Leicester's reactions. Besides, Virginia felt she wanted a nice peaceful night.

Leicester's mother had tea all ready when Virginia ar-

rived. She was a lovely cook. Virginia found her climb –
and possibly the stirring up of her emotions – had given
her a rare appetite. She did full justice to the delicious
bacon-and-egg pie, flanked with stuffed tomatoes, and the
feather-light jelly sponge that followed it. As Virginia took
her second cup of tea she said, 'Did Leicester tell you of
the comical turn his managers' meeting took on Tuesday
night?'

Mrs. Gordon had a smooth pale face, with thin lips that
were rather at variance with her somewhat heavy, though
undeniably handsome features and the expression of great
geniality that usually wreathed her face. But now these thin
lips narrowed still more and she shot a sideways glance at
Virginia.

'Did you get a letter this morning?'

'Yes, at work.'

'I thought you got one Saturday?'

'So I did,' returned Virginia, for no reason at all feeling
extraordinarily guilty, 'but I usually get at least one more
a week besides the Saturday one.'

Mrs. Gordon pursed her lips and changed the subject.
At least one more! Yet Leicester wrote her, his *mother*,
once a week. She had somehow not supposed Leicester's
feelings for Virginia as ardent as that. Especially as he
hated letter-writing anyway.

'Is Nancy coming round?' asked Virginia. She loved
Nancy. She would make the most perfect sister-in-law.

'Yes, but not till after eight. Geoffrey was getting home
later tonight. We'll be able to have a cosy little chat before
she arrives.'

For some reason Virginia thought that sounded ominous.
How ridiculous ... it was just that she was all on edge
tonight.

Mrs. Gordon made up the fire. Virginia took out her
knitting and her hostess her tatting. Mrs. Gordon achieved
the impossible and assumed an even more bland expression.

'I can't tell you how happy I am that you and Leicester
are settling down so nicely together.'

Virginia bent her head over her knitting. She said nothing. She would have preferred to have waited till Leicester had actually proposed before accepting any felicitations. Still, it was all in the family, she supposed, and she probably ought to be grateful for this approval, but she did not like this being taken for granted. Mrs. Gordon must think there was no chance of her refusing Leicester.

'It's *so* necessary for a minister to pick his wife with due care,' continued Mrs. Gordon. 'You know the ropes so well, being a daughter of the Manse. I told Leicester that long before he ever took you out. You're used to entertaining all manner of people and making ends meet on not too large a salary.'

Virginia decided to take it lightly. She chuckled, 'I don't think many ministers think of that when they pick their wives, Mrs. Gordon – they're probably just the same as any other man then, and obey their hearts rather than their heads. Which is what most of us want to be chosen for, I suppose.'

She thought to herself, a little indignantly, that it would be nothing less than an insult to be chosen for your suitability, for your adaptability. Just imagine it!

Mrs. Gordon sighed. 'Well, I daresay most girls cherish these romantic notions ... perhaps you, especially, with writing fiction. But I always think that marriages based on a good firm friendship, with two people in much the same walk of life, last far better than these whirlwind courtships.'

Virginia felt a wave of the same anger that had possessed her so disastrously a few hours ago pulse in her veins again. This was rubbing off the magic bloom with a vengeance!

Certainly nobody could call Leicester's courtship whirlwind – indeed Virginia hadn't looked for that – yet she knew that she, Virginia Jane Fergusson, wouldn't marry a man unless she were head over heels in love with him. Because if you weren't there was always the danger that somewhere, some time, you would meet someone for whom you would feel just that. To cover her feelings she chuckled again.

'Oh, I think you need the firm foundation of friendship, all right, Mrs. Gordon. You need to like a man as well as to love him, but you need something else too. Something that will stand through all sorts of adversity ... the something that has always existed between Mother and Father.'

Virginia would have liked to have added: 'The sort of thing that makes them still meet as lovers if they've had a couple of days apart ... a sort of unquenchable spark ...' but you just didn't say things like that to Mrs. Gordon. There was no poetry in the woman. She was so much a creature of sound common sense that everything else was crowded out ... you just couldn't imagine Mrs. Gordon ever going into raptures over a full moon or chasing rainbows! She looked across at her.

Mrs. Gordon's lips had tightened again. Virginia was well aware of the fact that Mrs. Gordon did not like Mrs. Fergusson. She wondered, not for the first time, if her mother had had Mrs. Gordon in mind when she had said once, with a twinkle, 'You have more trouble in the parish with the women who imagine *they* would have made perfect helpmeets for the minister than any others. They see it only as a position of social eminence and don't realize that side of it means less than nothing. It's your attitude in the home that counts and, as all wives find out, how happy you make your husband. Of course with these critical people the only cure would be to have them become ministers' wives – then they'd become tolerant, develop their sense of humour, learn to turn the other cheek, and suffer fools gladly.'

She realized that while she had been thinking this, Mrs. Gordon had given a slight snort at the mention of the bond between her father and mother and was sweeping on. 'Leicester's *always* been guided by me, of course. Right from a little lad I've had his fullest confidence. That's how I've been able to steer him clear of drifting into anything unsuitable—'

It was too much for Virginia ... she had an instant impish vision of Leicester narrowly avoiding the wiles of scores of glamour girls and near-Bohemians and tried, but didn't succeed, to choke back a giggle.

Mrs. Gordon said thinly, 'Have I said something amusing, Virginia?'

'No – o,' Virginia managed to say, 'just – I – I can't imagine Leicester involved with anyone – er—'

Mrs. Gordon said coldly, 'You haven't known Leicester *all* your life, Virginia. It might surprise you to know that you owe it to me that Leicester was still unattached when he met you.'

Virginia stared, then she laughed. 'Oh, I suppose we all have our teenage fancies. I never thought I was the first girl Leicester took out.'

There was a little silence, during which time Virginia felt herself suddenly aware that Mrs. Gordon was taking pleasure in deflating her. She wanted her son to marry her, yes, but she didn't want any girl to think Leicester adored her. Virginia went cold. Mrs. Gordon permitted herself a small, knowing smile. 'It wasn't a teenage fancy. He had already met you. And I recognized you as much more suitable than this other one he'd gone overboard for.'

Immediately Virginia went hot. Oh dear, what a day and night! She decided to keep a rein on her temper this time. This wasn't Leicester's fault. In fact, she thought it would be a good deed on her part to rescue him from his mama, and at least they would be a hundred miles away.

Mrs. Gordon lost the gleam of spitefulness and flowed on, 'But of course a bachelor minister is gravely hampered in his work. He just can't do the entertaining. He was saying to me just three months ago that the ladies' side of the work is not all he'd like it to be. They lack leadership. That's where your background would help.'

Virginia knew she was supposed to look grateful for this praise, so she managed what she hoped would pass for a pleased smile. She was vastly relieved when the door opened and Nancy breezed in and dropped a kiss on her mother's snowy hair.

'Geoff was early after all, so while I washed the dishes

he bathed the brats and I left him telling them their bedtime stories.'

Mrs. Gordon was not pleased at the interruption. She shook her head sorrowfully. 'When I was a young matron I'd never have dreamed of dropping my responsibilities like that. In fact your father never once had to bath you children.'

It didn't worry Nancy. She thought her mother rather a joke. 'Come off it, Mum. I bet you wished he had. I'm all for the modern male. Dad would have enjoyed our childhood much more if he'd been allowed to do things for us. Geoff just loves their bath-time. Heavens, what would have happened to me if he hadn't been able to do these things that time I broke my ankle and you were in Australia? If Geoff hadn't been used to changing and feeding the baby it would have been a nightmare. He even washed Pam's nappies the first few days.'

Mrs. Gordon sighed, then she changed the subject. 'I was having a heart-to-heart talk with Virginia about her settling down with Leicester. I was just telling her I think she'll make an ideal wife for a minister.'

Nancy cocked a quizzical brow at Virginia. 'Things just come to a head? Has Leicester been down? Oh, no, he'd have come to see me if he had. Did he propose by letter?'

Before Virginia could reply, Mrs. Gordon did. 'Well – well, nothing formal, but still ... it's a foregone conclusion. And of course Virginia and I get on so well together. You know just a year ago Leicester got so tired of boarding, even though it's in the Manse and they let him have a couple of rooms. And they told him that now they were established in the garage business they were thinking of building in Greenhaughs. Leicester said goodness knows what kind of tenants they'd get in the Manse next and asked me to go up there to keep house for him when they moved.

'Of course I couldn't. It's so large. Leicester knows what a high standard of housekeeping I go in for and he fondly imagined, silly boy, I could keep it up in that size house. I mean – those stairs! And all those acres of polished floors.

They have to be just polished – it would cost a small fortune to do them wall-to-wall – and what's the good in a manse where you have to move on? Leicester won't be in a small country parish for ever, mark my words. Where was I? Oh, yes. Well, I said to Leicester that at my age I couldn't possibly cope with the endless stream of callers, the telephone, the constant calls upon one's time, but then he said – you know how devoted he is to me, always putting me first – he said he didn't like to think of me living here alone – that the time was coming when I'd have to do something about that.'

Nancy said: 'Good heavens, Mum, you've not exactly got one foot in the grave. Why, lots of women your age are working. You know—'

Her mother said: 'Nancy! If your father could hear you! I'm not one of these career women. I led a sheltered life from the time I married him. And don't interrupt. So I told Leicester then – because I could see he was getting interested in Virginia – that I'd wait till he was married. That's one thing about these big old manses, there's always plenty of room. So see how right I was. Virginia is younger and more able than I . . . and so domesticated. And she could take all these things in her stride.'

Above Mrs. Gordon's head, bent over her tatting, Nancy's eyes met Virginia's. Her eyebrows had risen like twin peaks and though she gave Virginia a comical, bantering look, Virginia could sense an indignation in her second only to her own.

All unknowing, Mrs. Gordon went on. 'She could help Leicester with the parish work . . . teaching in the Sunday-school or leading a Bible class, or something, and I could pull my weight . . . in so far as my health allows. Setting tables and cleaning silver and so on. And to make up for leaving all my friends here I could probably do a little visiting with Leicester. You probably wouldn't like that side of parish work, I'd say, Virginia. You love to stay home and scribble, don't you?

'That's another thing. Your writing will be a great help.

Your mother was telling me how much you made out of free-lance stories and poetry last year. Ministers' stipends these days are quite good, but they have to be stretched to cover so much an ordinary household wouldn't know about. But of course as a minister's wife you'll have to be a little more circumspect. That story in the *Journal* last week, "She took the Plunge", was a little – well, a little raw, wasn't it?'

Virginia let a laugh escape her. She couldn't help it. 'You ought to see the ones I do under pseudonyms,' she said.

Well, didn't it sound entrancing? ... How nice to have one's life so neatly planned! The young and strong and domesticated wife doing all the heavy work, helping with the organizing and staying home while her husband and his mother partook of afternoon tea and were regaled with stories of pioneer days ... visiting was really a very happy hunting-ground for copy.

Mrs. Gordon said uncertainly, 'Well, that one ought to have been under a pseudonym. I wouldn't like to have seen that under Virginia Gordon, for instance. In fact I'm surprised your father didn't object. Or didn't you show it to him before you submitted it? It might be a good idea when you're married to show all you write to Leicester and—'

Virginia struck in with a surprising (to Mrs. Gordon) fierceness.

'Mrs. Gordon, my world of writing is mine alone! I write to please myself ... and a few editors. I live every moment of every word. And it expresses *my* personality, nobody else's. And never will.'

This statement was succeeded by a complete silence. Nancy felt she wanted to cheer, but dared not.

Virginia knitted calmly on ... she purled two, knitted two, purled two and came to the end of the row. She thrust the spare needle through the golden-yellow ribbing with an air of finality and stood up.

Her hair was a copper flame in the glow from a standard lamp, her face very white.

'I've found all you said very interesting, Mrs. Gordon,

26

and it would have been even more so supposing Leicester *had* asked me to marry him. Ever hear of "the famous Betty Baxter, who refused a man before he axed her," Mrs. Gordon?'

There was no answer.

Virginia continued: 'That's exactly what I'm doing. I haven't the least intention of marrying Leicester, and even if I had, while I hope I would make a reasonably good daughter-in-law I certainly would not commit the folly of starting off the very beginning of my married life in a household of three. That's the very thing my mother and father always advise against. Unless it's unavoidable, because of illness, they always say to any couple, if it's only a couple of rooms, they must be on their own.'

Nancy's eyes brimmed with tears, though inwardly she was applauding. She hadn't thought Virginia had it in her and had been rather worried at her mother's manipulation of the situation long since.

Mrs. Gordon's mouth fell open and stayed open.

With the promptness of a stage cue, the front door bell rang. Nancy went to answer it, inwardly fuming. She was back in a moment, terrified she might miss something. Her mother had managed to close her mouth and seemed to be swallowing and seeking for words. Virginia was standing there, very aloof, very straight and still.

Nancy said in a sort of hushed whisper, almost an awed one, 'It's your boss, Mr. Leslie Warrington. He says he wants to see you urgently, Virginia.'

Virginia turned and smiled, and to Nancy's amazement there was sheer deviltry in it. 'Tell him I've no wish to see him and that as far as I'm concerned, the incident is closed.'

Nancy goggled and disappeared.

'What,' said Mrs. Gordon faintly, 'is all this about?'

'Nothing,' said Virginia airily.

Nancy reappeared. 'He says he'll wait and take you home, Virginia, and he added – and meant it if I'm any judge – that he'd wait till midnight if need be!'

Virginia waved a hand dismissingly. 'Tell him I'm definitely *not* going home with him and that when I do go, it will be by taxi!'

Hugely enjoying herself, even if mystified, Nancy returned to the front door. The two left in the room heard voices a little raised, a guffaw from a man's voice, an uncertain giggle from Nancy's, and suddenly Les Warrington was in the room, tall, dark, debonair, twinkling.

'Excuse me,' he said to Mrs. Gordon, 'but I simply have to see Miss Fergusson tonight.' He turned to Virginia. 'You just can't do this to us – to me – Virginia. I've been round to see your mother and father and they told me where you were.'

'That's family loyalty for you,' said Virginia lightly. 'And what a nerve on your part!'

'I thought that by now you might have cooled off.'

'I have.' Virginia was very demure. 'In fact recent events have put it completely out of my mind – or had till you came in.'

Les looked vastly relieved. 'Thank heaven! Then you'll be back tomorrow morning as usual.'

Virginia shook her bright head. 'Oh, no. Whatever gave you that idea? I'm off for pastures new tomorrow morning.'

Mrs. Gordon and Nancy watched as if they were spectators of a film.

'Darling!' said Les suddenly and with warmth. He went across to her, taking her by the elbows. 'It was only a storm in a teacup and, as I said to you then, it only precipitated matters.

'I'm in deadly earnest. Come on, be matey. You don't need to give me your answer now . . . if you capitulate about leaving, it need not commit you to anything personal – but do give me a chance to make you take back that very positive no you gave me when you were so flaming mad with my mother this afternoon. You can't be still angry with *me*, surely?'

Virginia shook her head. She had a curiously detached air, still rather pale, but her eyes were as green as a witch's.

'*You* did nothing to anger me. After all, what's a kiss?'

Mrs. Gordon's mouth fell open again.

Leslie gave Virginia a good shake. 'That kiss, as I told you, you little devil, was the forerunner of a proposal of marriage.'

'Yes, I know,' innocence just oozed from Virginia. 'But I refused you, didn't I?'

'Oh, hell!' said Leslie Warrington, then laughed. 'The trouble is you're not taking me seriously.'

'Oh yes, I am! You made me an offer – seriously. I'm turning it down – seriously.' Her lips twitched, her eyes danced and suddenly laughter had its way with her.

'That's better,' approved Les. 'And now you can think it over again ... still more seriously. To England for our honeymoon – wouldn't you just love that? Then back here. Any site in Dunedin to build a house on. Or if you want an old house, well, that will be okay by me. You like old things, don't you?'

All Les's promises made, by and large, quite a packet. ...

When he had finished Virginia said dryly, 'The stalled ox, in fact. Those things don't really matter, Les, you colossal idiot! Probably I'm an incurable romantic – but I like being that way – but better a dinner of herbs where love is, and all that!'

Les's mischievous face suddenly became grave. 'It would be where love is, Virginia, and you damned well know it. After all, the cottages don't have the monopoly of love. People have even known an ideal love in palaces—' for the first time he appeared conscious of an audience and embarrassed. 'Look, we can't talk here – get your coat on, girl, and we'll go some place private. I've talked to your father about this.'

'What?' Virginia lost her detached and maddening air of amusement. 'Good lord! What did Daddy say?'

Les grinned. 'That there was someone else in the running, but that needn't stop me ... go ahead and let the best man win. You know, I honestly did think that you trotted that out for sheer self-defence against Mother this afternoon.

I've never noticed any lover-boy hanging round the staff entrance!'

'You couldn't,' retorted Virginia, goaded. 'He doesn't live in Dunedin.'

'Oh, I see. Anyway, your papa added that having known you for twenty-four years he was perfectly sure you would please yourself without any approval or disapproval from your father.'

'And so I will. But at the present moment I wouldn't consider *any* man unless he was a foundling, brought up in an orphanage without a relation in the world!'

She looked straight at Mrs. Gordon who had tried so very hard to make Virginia see her duty to Leicester, his career and his manse. For the first time Virginia's look was bitter. Despite all her brave defiance her world seemed to be crumbling about her.

She suddenly felt she couldn't bear any more. She turned to Nancy. 'Would you get my coat and bag? They're in the spare room.'

Mrs. Gordon decided to see if her legs would support her. It *is* disconcerting when the girl you imagined would make a docile and suitable bride for your son suddenly turns into a – a volcano, with strange – and wealthy – young men bursting into your home, demanding to see her, and proposing marriage. She moistened her lips.

'Virginia,' she said imploringly, without a hint of blandness, 'would you come round and see me tomorrow after you've had a good sleep?'

Virginia shook her head. 'I won't have time. I'm leaving on the North Express at midday tomorrow.'

Mrs. Gordon sat down again.

Nancy brought the coat, watched while Les held it for Virginia and buttoned it round her, smiling down on her. A smile that Virginia did not return. She went to the door with them. She squeezed Virginia's hand, pulling her back a little. 'Good for you,' she whispered, 'you'll have Mother eating out of your hand after this!'

Back in the room Mrs. Gordon had her hand to her heart, which didn't worry Nancy a scrap since she knew perfectly well there was nothing whatever wrong with her mother's heart. But Mrs. Gordon did have a dew of perspiration on her brow.

'Nancy,' she said pathetically, 'surely I must have dreamt all this?'

'I think you started it, really,' Nancy said slowly. 'Rather like sowing the wind and reaping the whirlwind.'

At the look on her mother's face, Nancy sat down and gave way to the mirth that had been threatening her for ages. It was either that, or cry.

Her mother regarded her reproachfully. 'How you can find any humour in the situation, I just don't know.'

Nancy wiped her eyes and endeavoured to look serious. 'It – it – was just too much for me. I mean I never dreamed Virginia had it in her. I'd never suspected Virginia was interested in anyone but Leicester. He'll have to sit up. My little brother is too used to having things drop in his lap. He has potentialities of personality he doesn't bother to develop. After all, what's an inconvenient manse and a back-country parish got to compare with a trip to England and a mansion on Maori Hill?'

Mrs. Gordon bleated, 'But if she loves Leicester—'

Nancy broke in, unrebuked for interruption this time. 'It sounded to me as if she wanted to be convinced that *Leicester* loved *her*. You made it sound just as if it were a marriage of convenience, Mother. Just as if Leicester was considering her as a housekeeper and sort of unpaid assistant. No girl wants to be married for that. What a lovely hair-do she'd had.'

Mrs. Gordon waved away the question of the hair-do impatiently, but took the strictures in a surprisingly meek fashion. She sounded most uneasy.

'Nancy, you do think when she's slept on it that she'll come round to see me, don't you? I could apologize. You don't think she'll stay angry and fly off to the ends of the earth, do you?'

'Oh, she probably can't afford to go as far as that – although you never know. Some girls do go to England on a working holiday – but I should think Wellington or Auckland. Still, you never know with these redheads, once they're aroused. I always thought Virginia was far too placid for her colouring. But oh dear, her performance tonight! She had that gorgeous man just eating out of her hand! *He'd* go to any girl's head. Poor Leicester! Of course, she might go to Australia. Hasn't she got an aunt in Sydney?'

'But what am I to say to Leicester?' wailed Mrs. Gordon. 'And I was only trying to speed things on.'

Nancy sobered. 'Mother, I think you've got to be honest – if you want to get anywhere, and if you don't want to estrange your son. Admit you were trying to get yourself settled in. You know, pet, you'll let yourself become an old lady long before your time, if you continue like this. You need a new attitude of mind and a few new interests. Plenty of things for you to do – charitable organizations would be glad of your time.'

Mrs. Gordon said miserably, 'I still don't know what I'm going to say to Leicester. I mean if Virginia writes to him – she's bound to write – she may put me in such a bad light. I'd like to tell him my intentions were the best.'

Nancy reflected, but was too kind to say, that good intentions had proverbially paved the way to hell. She wanted to comfort her mother, but this was the time, she felt, to scare seven bells out of her and stop her trying to live her children's lives. So she said reflectively, 'M'mm. It's going to make Leicester think a bit, isn't it? I mean, if he ever suspected that it was you who persuaded Melanie to give him up, and added that to tonight's fiasco, it wouldn't make him – well, very kindly disposed towards you.'

Mrs. Gordon turned pale. 'Nancy, you wouldn't ever tell him I went to see Melanie, would you?'

Nancy said, 'No, I certainly wouldn't. But I'd always hoped – till Virginia came along – that you'd have told him yourself one day. That you persuaded Melanie she'd never make a minister's wife.'

Mrs. Gordon said pleadingly, 'Nancy, you know what she was like? A flibbertigibbet. Mad on clothes.'

'That's not a crime, Mother. Melanie would have toed the line in that when she got married; we all do.'

'But you do think Virginia is the ideal one for Leicester? With her behind him, Leicester would reach the top, I'm sure. Her father is such an influence in the Church, he's in very good standing.'

Nancy made a face of distaste. 'Oh, Mother, don't talk like that! It sounds a rat-race and it was never meant to be that. Mr. Fergusson is so unassuming. He only thinks of service, not of position. And I'm of the opinion that a man isn't worth very much – in any position – if he needs a woman of strong character behind him. I always felt – I could be wrong, of course – that because Melanie was the clinging type, it would be good for Leicester, because she would lean on him – not the other way round. I feel Melanie would rouse all the best, protective instincts in Leicester.' Suddenly tears shone in Nancy's eyes. 'I – I – I've always felt that something went out of Leicester's life when Melanie gave him up. I felt terribly worried about my brother for months and months, even if Virginia is more of a kindred spirit, as far as I'm concerned, than Mel was. And I wonder now if that's why Virginia is restless. Oh, I think she loves Leicester . . . but she's conscious of needing more from him than she gets. Perhaps ardour. Now don't look at me as if I was mentioning something indecent, Mother. There's got to be ardour between a man and wife. And I reckon darling Virginia has plenty of doubts. And she's never known about Mel. I reckon that wasn't right.

'Well, we can't do anything about it right now, dear. But tell you what I'll do tomorrow morning. I'll ring Leicester long distance, and tell him – I'll play your part down as much as I can without being unfair to Virginia, and tell him, and perhaps he could see Virginia at Oamaru. The express stops there twenty minutes or so for lunch at the refreshment rooms.

'You know, Mother, it won't hurt Leicester to have to

exert himself to win Virginia. Most things have come to him too easily. He didn't even have to sweat and slave at the wool-stores or the freezing-works to help put himself through college like most of the divinity students had to – you made it all too easy for him. But now with the wealthy and fascinating Les Warrington in the running he'll have to wake up. Leicester has got it in him, but he's been pampered.'

Normally Nancy wouldn't have dared speak like this to her mother, but with Leicester's and Virginia's happiness at stake she felt she must.

'Now I'm going to get a taxi and take you home with me for the night. I'll give you a hot drink and a couple of aspirins and you'll feel a whole heap better in the morning.'

To her complete surprise, her mother turned it down. 'I'd rather be here in case Virginia rings me, after she gets home.'

Nancy looked doubtful. 'I think Les Warrington had other ideas. I heard him say as they went down the path, "Thus far I've had two audiences for my proposals . . . but this time the only witness is going to be that moon!"'

Mrs. Gordon's only answer was a moan.

The Fergussons' manse was in a lovely terrace overlooking the Bay. Mr. Fergusson served the church here and two other smaller bays. But Les didn't take the valley road that led up to the Manse, he swung the car on to a car park perched above the rocks.

It was a perfect night, dark waves rolling up the curving beach and creaming into froth at the edge, lights all around the harbour, indented goldenly into all the little bays, twinkling remotely on the over-harbour hills where there were farmsteads, and the carpet of white and yellow radiance where the city lay on her hills.

Les turned to Virginia. 'So far I've not had much of a show, but here's the right setting, I think. I've proposed once in front of my mother and once in front of – what was the smooth lady's name?'

Virginia's eyes danced. 'Oh, just refer to her as my former prospective mother-in-law!'

'What? Oh, my God!' Les was really startled. 'Then it was true. I thought you'd made him up. I say, I didn't mean—'

'Oh, don't worry, Les. I'd already wiped that – about three minutes before you forced your way in. I've *had* mothers-in-law – at least prospective ones. We were right in the middle of a real donnybrook when you came in. Mrs. Gordon was the last straw in a hateful, if exciting day, for me! And I'm a bit sick of proposals. As you say, you've proposed twice in front of witnesses – well, I've had worse than that, believe me . . . I've been proposed to, for the man I love, *by his mother!* And if that wouldn't kill romance, what would?'

Les stared, then he guffawed. Virginia joined in. 'It's not funny really,' she choked. 'I've lost my job and I'm leaving the home I adore and you're at outs with your mother, and I don't know what Leicester Gordon will say to his . . . and I ought to be broken-hearted – and all I'm doing is *giggling*. I feel cheated. Perhaps I'm not the stuff romance is made of, after all!'

Les sobered up and said, 'Virginia, you are! You just got tied up with the wrong man, that's all. So it's just as well it happened. Because you're going to marry me, do you hear? Now sober up. I admit neither you nor I have had a fair go till now, but what could be more perfect than this?' He waved a hand. 'Here's the time, the place, and the loved one all together . . . deserted beach, a dream of a moon, even soft music!'

They both laughed as the strains of a guitar came across the waters to them, from a cottage on the other side of the beach.

'All right,' said Virginia cruelly. 'It's as good a setting as any in which to offer to be a sister to you.'

Les ignored her. There was a little track that led down to the beach. Les helped her down, going first, and at the foot swung her down, putting his cheek against hers before he put her down on the soft sand.

The breeze from the sea cooled Virginia's hot temples and blew the coppery strands of hair loose above her forehead. It would probably be the end of that hair-set, and good riddance to it too. Salt spray and hair spray didn't mix. It went sticky. She watched the moon obscure itself behind a dreamy bar of cloud, 'Very discreet, that moon,' said Les.

She wondered what arguments he'd use now. But he was very wise. And knew a fair bit about women.

He kissed her instead. When he stopped kissing her Virginia knew she had softened. There was something very nice about Les. He was boyish and mischievous and rather ingenuous.

'Well,' he said now, 'rather nice, wasn't it?'

'Yes, but it doesn't mean a thing,' said Virginia.

'I'm not taking no for an answer, darling,' he said to the top of her head.

'I don't see what else you can do – short of abduction. And there's no Gretna Green in New Zealand.'

Finally, still confident, he took her back to the Manse. As he left her he said, 'Does it have to be one to kiss and one to turn the cheek? After all, as you said to the smooth lady – incidentally, I reckon my mother would make a far more agreeable mother-in-law than her – as you said to her, what's in a kiss?'

Suddenly Virginia found it all gorgeous and lighthearted fun. She raised herself up by his arms, and kissed him, full on the mouth, but lightly.

In view of that kiss, Leslie Warrington was very surprised when Virginia was absent from the office next morning.

CHAPTER THREE

VIRGINIA awoke to find her mother coming into the room with a breakfast tray.

'Gracious,' she said sleepily, 'it's not late, is it?'

'Very late,' said her mother tranquilly, sitting on the edge of the bed and offering baked gurnet with parsley sauce. 'In fact it's nine-thirty. Les Warrington has just rung to speak to you. I've told him you can't possibly spare the time, you're busy packing.

'Listen, Virginia, as soon as you get up, have your bath but don't get dressed – just put a brunch coat on – I've some things coming up from Smyrnington's for you to try on. A little gift from Father and me to wish you luck.'

Tears came into Virginia's eyes as she put the tray to one side and took her mother's face lovingly between her hands. 'Oh, Mother, did ever a girl have a mother like you? Or a father like Dad? Some fathers, particularly, would have been horrified at all the kerfuffle I caused yesterday. Some would have said I'd been foolish, walking out on a good job, or rated me soundly for paying so much attention to Mrs. Gordon's ideas on rules for marriage, might have made me feel foolish and impetuous. But neither of you uttered a word of reproach, just told me it was time I left the nest and experienced some other life than this. Oh, I do love you both!'

Mrs. Fergusson smiled. She had a rich, rare beauty. Her hair was chestnut where Virginia's was red, and her eyes brown, not green. Pansy eyes, her husband called them.

'Well, Virginia, I feel you've reached a crisis period in your life, and I'm almost glad. You were simply drifting. I've felt for some time you were almost too content with things as they are. And to go from one manse existence to another is something I don't want for you – yet. I'd like you to know something different before you make any irrevocable decisions. I've found manse life more than worth while because of your father, but there was a freedom about my girlhood you've never known. The parishioners have always had to be considered first. I want you to have a bit of a fling before you settle down.' She grinned. 'Within reasonable bounds, of course!'

She paused. 'You know, Virginia, I've never forgotten that when your father's eyesight failed and he had to have that expensive operation in America, you gave up your university career and took on shop work, even though you loathed it at first. But it tided us over. We can't give you those years back, Virginia, but we've put aside regularly for the last year or two a certain sum each month that was to be used for your trousseau if you needed one.

'When you said last night you'd like to get a flat in Christchurch and try to make your living by free-lancing, we felt we'd like to help. We'd like you to have a little bank balance behind you till you get a bunch of acceptances, so you can work with your mind free from worry, and I want you to have some super clothes, lots of them.

'There's nothing like the feeling of being well-dressed to give you confidence, and if you want to go about storming editors' offices and what not, I'd like you to look the part.'

Virginia burst out laughing. 'I don't know about the storming, Mother, most of my assaults will be per bulky envelopes – much better policy than personal interviews. They'll only be interested in my manuscripts, not me, but I'll love having the clothes. Bless you, darling!'

Mrs. Fergusson replaced the tray, uncovered the fish again, and said, 'Now eat up, then scoot for the bathroom. I'll turn the bath on slowly. And I promised Penny – I told her an edited version of your story at breakfast – that we'll call in at the Bay School and say goodbye to her.'

Smyrnington's delivery van was at the gate before Virginia was out of the bath. The young assistant from the showroom who accompanied the boxes was thrilled to help Virginia.

She chose a duck-egg three-piece jersey suit, a filmy

black formal frock, a green crêpe wool, flecked with metallic gold, and some new sweaters and trews. For travelling in there was a hunting green suede coat, loosely belted across the back, with a two-piece matching tweed suit for underneath it, and a suede jerkin. It was fittingly called the Sherwood Model.

When accessories came tumbling out, shoes, bag, gloves, hats, a padded nylon brunch coat in pure turquoise with shortie pyjamas to match, Virginia said: 'Oh, Mother, I just can't take all this!' But her mother refused to be badgered into returning them. 'Don't deny me a great pleasure, Virginia,' she said, and lifted out a sapphire velvet evening coat. 'I want you to go to operas and the ballet, recitals and plays, and not count the cost. I want you to have the sort of gaiety I had years ago. Not that I ever hanker for it now, but I might have, had I never had it.

'And your father has a cheque for you. He's been busy too – he's rung Christchurch and booked you in for a few days at the Clarendon Hotel. That will give you time to look round Christchurch for a flat. You'll love it there. It overlooks the Avon.'

Just before they left Nancy rang. 'Are you really serious about going North today, Virginia?' Not a word that she had already rung Leicester and warned him Virginia might, then had waited, hoping Virginia might ring to say she had changed her mind.

'Yes, I'm going, Nancy. I'm just getting ready and I haven't too much time and we've got to call in to say good-bye to Penny. Now I hate to rush this call, but I'll have to, but I'll write to you, Nancy. *You've* been a darling. And listen, there'll be a little news item in the paper tonight. No, I'm not being mysterious, only it would take too long to tell you now. I'll have to fly, the car's at the door and Father's at the horn! Good-bye, Nan.'

Nancy rang Leicester again.

Les was at the station. He had hired her a pillow and there was a soft plaid rug from the travel department lying on the seat. That was very thoughtful ... and chosen with care, because it was in the soft greens of the Fergusson tartan. He put a pile of the newest overseas magazines on the rack and a box of chocolates and he had a colourful box he kept to the last with Florista Ltd. printed on it in gold lettering. His eyes approved the suit, the jaunty hat.

'Good morning, Maid Marian,' he said, recognizing the Sherwood model of the rival firm with a grin. Virginia grinned back. It was somehow satisfying to appear for once in something not sponsored by Warrington and Son.

'I'll give you a fortnight exactly,' said Les, 'then I'll pop up by plane and put the question to you again.'

Impish lights danced in Virginia's eyes. 'Make it a month and I might have had time to miss you,' she said audaciously.

Mrs. Fergusson decided Les Warrington was a most endearing lad. Who knew? Perhaps Virginia was not as indifferent as she looked. Perhaps she had the sense now to make the going harder for Les than she had for Leicester. Mrs. Fergusson approved of that. She had always felt Virginia had been just a little too lacking in the art of coquetry.

Virginia had a sense of adventure as the train pulled out. She had never before been free to do anything like this, she had known financial responsibility so long. It had taken the Fergusson family a long time to recover from the expense of Father's illness and the family had remained closely-knit to accomplish this.

Virginia had a window seat and she leaned back to gaze restfully on the coastline, green and blue, below her. Then at Katiki they ran close to the surf-shore where golden sands and wind-tossed surf made the day golden and blue. They wouldn't reach Christchurch till after seven when the express would halt for tea refreshments, then go on under the Port Hills to Lyttelton where the North Island-bound passengers would board the all-night steamer ferry for Wellington.

She was hungry by the time they got to Oamaru and the lunch stop. As she swung off the train she felt her elbow clutched. She turned, looked up. Leicester! Virginia's heart skipped a beat in the traditional manner. A wave of love for him swept over her. But no hint of this was allowed to show.

Leicester thought he had never seen Virginia look so lovely. She was usually such a tomboy, with coppery locks wind-tossed or hurriedly smoothed down. But today there wasn't a tress out of place – she'd had something done to it, he wasn't sure what, and Les Warrington's violets and primroses were lovely on the green suit.

Leicester said firmly, 'We're going to have a talk, Virginia, in my car. It's parked just outside.'

'I'm very hungry,' said Virginia. 'I didn't bother with even coffee at Palmerston.'

'Oh, I'll feed you while I talk. I've got it all under control.'

Virginia realized Nan must have rung him. She also knew without a shadow of doubt that despite her feeling for him, all his talking would not alter her decision one whit.

Leicester put her into the car. 'I'll be back in a moment, Virginia.'

She supposed he was after a cup of tea and a sandwich for her. A few moments later she heard the boot of the car slam, but was too busy planning what arguments she would use to wonder why. Leicester got in the seat beside her.

'I've just had the engine re-bored,' he said, 'deuced expensive, of course, but what a difference it's made. Engine just purrs . . . listen!'

Virginia knew another wave of feeling, but not one of love this time. She had made one of the most momentous decisions of her life – Nancy was bound to have told him all – and all he could talk about was car engines! Talk about the days of romance! Really, modern men deserved all they did not get! They deserved to be turned down flat, and she, for one, was going to enjoy doing just that! She was done with the lot of them.

Leicester put it into reverse and then shot forward, roaring up the street. He was two blocks south before Virginia found her voice. 'Leicester, don't be ridiculous! I'm not in the least interested in this beastly engine. I want something to eat and I want to take it back on the train with me. Where do you think you're taking me?'

'Oh, we can't talk in front of a dingy old railway station. No romance in that. There's lots of time, Virginia, and Oamaru has some lovely nooks.'

'I don't give a darn for lovely nooks *or* romance!' she said, completely forgetting her indignation at the lack of it a moment ago. 'All I'm concerned about is catching my train to Christchurch. You take me right back to that train now. This very moment!'

She might have been speaking to the great open spaces. Up the wide, tree-centred avenue that was Oamaru's main street, Thames Street, they went, and up Severn Street Hill, ablaze with creepers and flowers on its stone terraces below the houses.

Alarmed, Virginia sat bolt upright. 'This is too far. Leicester, stop! Where *do* you think we're going?'

Leicester's tone was nonchalant, but he was grinning. 'South to Maheno, then west to Greenhaughs.' He burst out laughing. 'Oh, Jinny, if you could only see your face!'

She sought for words.

He added, 'In short, my lass, you're abducted . . . thought it only happened in Regency days, didn't you? Won't it make good copy? Your next short story, I foresee, will have a flavour like this . . . wayward heroine abducted by the hero, saved from the consequences of her own folly. Up into the saddle with her, and off!'

Virginia panicked . . . that train would be within six or seven minutes of leaving. 'You idiot, Leicester! All my beautiful new clothes are on that train . . . what they cost Mother and Dad I dare not think – stop this car this very moment and go back!'

This had the strange effect of making the Reverend Leicester Gordon accelerate. 'Your luggage is in the boot, my love, safe and sound.'

Virginia's voice was icy. 'And what, may I ask, do you intend doing with me?'

'Well, first I'll feed you, since your hunger seems to be overlaying your sense of the romantic. And then I'll keep you to myself long enough to persuade you to marry me next month. You can look over the Manse while you're here. I told Mrs. Meredith that I was meeting the express and that I would probably be able to persuade you to break your journey.'

'Persuade!' said Virginia with biting sarcasm.

Leicester continued unperturbed. 'I also told her you'd probably stay the night. Nancy rang me this morning and told me the whole sad story of Mother's tactless remarks.'

He grinned reminiscently, but did not add that Nancy had gone on to say: 'And you'd better look to your laurels, my lad. I'd advise cave-man methods. Virginia's hopping mad and this Les Warrington is positively irresistible. Bags of money, too. I'm half in love with him myself. Mother has rubbed the gingerbread gilt off in no uncertain manner. You're going to have to work really hard convincing Virginia that you're head over heels in love with her. You've taken her far too much for granted. I expect you thought because she was a daughter of the manse, she'd like to become the mistress of a manse. In fact, my darling little brother, you're emotionally lazy. And that wouldn't satisfy any woman. So get cracking! Take your mind off your parish, off other people, and concentrate on Virginia!'

When Virginia did not reply, Leicester looked at her sideways and said: 'It's not possible for a chap's mother to interpret his feelings, you know, Jinny. So don't blame me for what Mother said.'

Suddenly Virginia was horrified to find she wanted to laugh . . . the whole thing was so darned unexpected, and if she laughed, Leicester would assume all was well, so she said, rather pettishly, 'And *don't* call me Jinny! It – it makes me feel like a – like an abigail! I can't bear it. I'm Virginia. I hate Jinny.'

43

His lips twitched. 'I can think of other things to call you besides Virginia . . . much nicer things.'

'I don't want to hear them,' said Virginia. 'I'm not in the mood. That was a first-class ticket I had . . . it's sheer waste.'

'You aren't going to need it, my love. You're going right back to Dunedin, tomorrow or the next day, and you're going to be extremely busy for the next few weeks getting your trousseau together.'

'Ever hear of the famous Betty Baxter—' Virginia began.

'Yes, I have. Just this morning. Nancy must have spent a fortune on that telephone call, bless her. Betty Baxter refused a man before he axed her, and all that, but that's not going to do me out of proposing to you, in any case.'

Virginia lapsed into what she hoped he'd take for a grim silence.

The lovely miles sped by. Virginia got hungrier still. And madder. But she wouldn't ask him to stop yet. To have to ask for food sort of took the edge off your dignity. If only she had had something at Palmerston!

When he drew up at Maheno she hoped for a tea-shop. But no, they were stopping at a cottage. 'I'm going in to get the key to this Anglican Church to show you. It's the one the Nichols family of Kuriheka built.'

Virginia gazed up at the church of red sandstone and decided she would like to see it, if she could forget the pangs that were gnawing at her. Leicester appeared from the cottage with an enormous key.

The church was dim and the light diffused through beautiful memorial windows. Virginia drew in a deep breath, tribute to the beauty of design and detail, and in releasing it, released also much of her anger. Which, of course, was exactly what she was meant to do. It was completely wrong to have thoughts of anger in a place of worship.

The whole place made her think of: 'Let us worship the Lord in the beauty of holiness.'

They walked together up the blue-carpeted aisle. She had a sudden thought of how lovely a setting it would make for a wedding ... if only weddings could be simple and private, a taking of vows by the two people concerned ... no fussing guests, no prickly confetti, no gigglings and whisperings. No mother-in-law looking martyred, as if one had committed all the crimes in the calendar by marrying her son.

Just two people standing before that beautiful altar, a white-haired, black-robed clergyman – yes, white hair would be essential – and two unknown witnesses. ...

There were native birds carved into the plain woods of the furnishings, memorial tablets that spoke poignantly of pioneer days when death by fire and flood were not uncommon. One of the men of the family had been killed in the accident that befell the last horse-drawn coach to cross the old Horse Range; 1878, that was.

Then there were the memorials to the many sons and grandsons of that family who had given their lives in two world wars.

They turned to the south wall. Here, set in the wall, were stone fragments brought to this tiny township in New Zealand, from some of the oldest cathedrals in England, the Mother-country. They traced out the inscriptions that ran squarely round them like a frame:

'These stones from ancient English shrines are placed here in the hope that the spirit which inspired their fashioning will also hallow these walls.'

Leicester read slowly the places the stones had come from: 'Canterbury, St. Paul's, London, Lichfield, Glastonbury, Westminster, Winchester.'

He paused. 'You remember that article you once wrote, Ji – Virginia, on Poetry and the Practical?'

She nodded, warily.

'This makes me think of that. This family designed all this beauty to minister to the beauty-loving side of us, but didn't forget the other needs, either. The wife of Colonel Cowie-Nichols also saw to it that here, where we get such a

45

light rainfall, and most houses depend on rain-water tanks, the river water was piped up into the village street.'

Virginia instantly sparkled. She got out the inevitable notebook, jotted it down and copied out the inscription around the stones. Her anger had completely deserted her. No doubt at all, Leicester was a kindred spirit. Need one ask more, look for more when choosing a life-partner?

He smiled down on her and said, 'Well, I've shown you the things of the spirit, Virginia, now for the practical. Let's find us a place to eat.'

They got back into the car and headed for the hills. It was gracious country, just as Leicester had described it to her in his letters – low, rolling hills, singing streams, willow bordered rivers, tussock-gold slopes and a patchwork effect where gorse hedges separated the paddocks.

Here, in a country where wooden buildings predominated, North Otago had the pleasant mellowness of weathered limestone stables and houses and even fences built of stone, survivals of pioneer days and patience.

Presently Leicester turned up a side lane, deeply rutted, and brought his car to a standstill where poplars and willows stood guard over a grassy-edged stream that gurgled happily over boulders.

The express, probably gathering speed across the Canterbury Plains now, seemed a million miles away. Leicester produced a snowy cloth begged from Mrs. Meredith, sandwiches, steaming coffee – had ever anything tasted so good? – and two apple-pies. 'I know they're your favourites, Virginia.'

Virginia dabbled her fingers in the stream, dried them on a handkerchief. There, now she was satisfied, she could think. She sat down on the rug, drew her knees up and clasped her hands round them. In the slim straight suit of Robin Hood green she looked as if she belonged. She looked up as Leicester tossed his cigarette into the stream and saw male appreciation in his eyes. He dropped down on to the rug, propped himself against a willow trunk and drew her against him.

'What's it all add up to, Virginia? Nan told me a great tale. What really happened? Did what happened at the shop upset you – so that you felt my mother's attitude was the last straw? What upset you most?'

Virginia would have preferred him not to be so disturbingly close. She'd got into the habit of being in love with Leicester. She would much rather have talked to him with her back against one of those trees, standing there nonchalantly and distantly. Not like this. Because your senses betrayed you at times like this. She wanted nothing more than to turn her head under his chin and be comforted. But she wouldn't.

So her tone, at least, was calm and faintly derisive. 'It's hard to define which upset me most, Leicester ... Martha Warrington catching Les kissing me ... that meant nothing, by the way. He simply took me unawares. He's always been a frightful flirt, even though at the moment he's trying to persuade me he's serious ... but perhaps I was more taken off balance by what your mother said.' All of a sudden she stopped, taken off balance again and thrown into confusion by an unwelcome awareness that neither of these things had hurt her as much as something else. Leicester looked at her searchingly. Then he shook her by the arm. 'What is it? Get it off your chest.'

She thought for a moment longer. 'Very well, but you won't like it ... I've just realized something. While it did sting when your mother took it for granted I'd marry you, and then proceeded to brush the stardust off our romance by insisting she had advised the match – that I was suitable, sensible, knew the ropes of parish life, and could even help a little financially with my writing, though she didn't want me writing anything at all – well, raw was the word she used – under *your* name! Well, as I said, I thought that had hurt most, but I was wrong. What really did hurt was that it only fed a conviction that's been growing on me for quite some time, only I didn't want to foster it ... that you've been very lukewarm, Leicester. That there could be

47

more than a grain of truth in what your mother said. I'm *suitable!* Ugh!

'No girl wants to be that. She wants a bit of romance, a bit of glamour. So suddenly I was scared. I was in danger of slipping into something that might not satisfy me.'

Well, if she had wanted reaction from Leicester she certainly got it. He stared at her quite incredulously. 'That might not satisfy you? Why, girl, of course I love you! Haven't I just abducted you to prove it?'

They measured glances, Leicester blinked. 'Do you know, I think you really *have* got doubts!'

Virginia said soberly, 'I think I've had them for a long time. I think I loved you just a bit too much for your own good, Leicester.'

Leicester shook her. 'You couldn't possibly love me too much! I want you to love me like that!'

Virginia pursed her lips. 'What I really mean, Leicester, is that I loved you more than you loved me – only I wouldn't face up to it . . . and I think there was more than a grain of truth in what your mother said.'

'Oh, bosh! Look, Virginia, I think perhaps I've been a little abstracted. Perhaps I let my work get between us a little. It can happen – it will be different when we're married. You—'

She held her hand up. 'Your work would always be with us – don't promise what you can't perform. Look, I've been to blame in this too – I thought it would be ideal, the sort of life I've been used to. Only I think a minister and his wife have to have the sort of bond that Mother and Dad have got, to make it stick. There's something lacking in our relationship – yours and mine. Otherwise I'm sure I could never have felt as I did last night, when Les Warrington took me home – I – oh, I almost despised myself, but it was suddenly gorgeous fun!' and Virginia dropped her eyes to hide the sudden gleam of sheer enjoyment that had shot into them, remembering, but she didn't do it quickly enough. Leicester had seen it. He stared. He'd never seen Virginia like this . . . provocative, intriguing.

She looked up, the gleam subdued, 'Anyway, Leicester, somehow or other, between Martha Warrington, your mother, and the sudden merciless analysing of my own feelings, I've discovered I have no ambition for marriage – yet. So if you were meaning to propose, Leicester, I'm refusing you.'

'Meaning to propose? What the dickens do you think I've been doing ever since we left Oamaru? I must be mad. There's only one answer to a discussion like this,' and he sprang to his feet and pulled her to hers. As his arms came round her, Virginia looked over his shoulder, gave a well-simulated start and said: 'There's a car coming,' and escaped.

Leicester had involuntarily looked round. 'Liar!' he said, and caught her again.

Virginia allowed herself no response, even though it took a lot of self-control, but she reflected bitterly that if he had kissed her like this before, none of this would have come to pass. He slackened his grip, looking down on her in a puzzled fashion.

She turned her hands outwards in a shrug. 'You see ... it didn't mean a thing. You and I have to do some very serious thinking, Leicester.'

There was a little smile at the back of his eyes. 'Well, we'll do it in the old Manse garden, Virginia, by the light of the stars. It's old and rambling and not very well kept, but there's a gate that opens on to a hillside. And if I remember there'll be a moon.'

Virginia said innocently, oh, much too innocently, 'Yes, there will be. It was full last night.'

Leicester put her into the car, much more attentively than he used to.

He said, as they drove on, 'Tonight we'll forget about everything and everyone. Thank heaven I've got no meeting. We've always been surrounded too much by our families – yours and mine. We'll have to be a bit more selfish, I think. Live our own lives.'

Virgnia felt a softening within her. To counteract it she

said sturdily, 'That was what we should have done long ago. It's been a very pedestrian sort of courtship, hasn't it?'

He said, 'Well, it won't be from now on, I promise.'

Virginia said, more sharply, 'I think you haven't got it straight, Leicester. Christchurch is much further from Greenhaughs than Dunedin was.'

Leicester looked startled. 'But you won't be going to Christchurch now, will you? Now we've had this talk.'

Virginia's brows drew together. 'Nothing has been altered – nothing at all. I'm all set for it. A new life. I want to spread my wings.'

Leicester laughed suddenly. 'Look, this is no place for arguing. I think we'd better leave it till we have a better setting. I'm sure the Manse garden and the moonlight will help my cause. This is so unlike you. You'll get over it, darling, and see things in your usual philosophical way soon.'

He patted her knee.

Was he too complacent? Too sure he could cope with this bit of feminine perversity? Too sure she cared enough for him to let things slip back into the old comfortable groove, with no fireworks, no temperament? Was he banking on the chance of himself and the moonlight proving an irresistible combination? Virginia had more than a suspicion they might at that!

She looked desperately out at the lovely countryside unfolding before her . . . homesteads with avenues of English trees leading up to them, a little humpy-backed bridge at a bend in the road, a stone stable with dormer windows, and fleecy clouds in a perfect sky. It wasn't fair. She so loved the country. They crested a hill and saw across the next bridge the township of Greenhaughs. Virginia knew a moment of panic. She was getting stampeded into capitulating and Leicester would sink back into taking her for granted once he was sure of her again.

The words were jerked out of her. 'Leicester, that other girl – the one you loved before you met me? You went

50

overboard for her, didn't you? Is that why you weren't swept off your feet for me?'

It didn't need his instant recoil, his involuntary 'Melanie' or the tightening of his hands on the wheel, to give Virginia her answer. She thought she had known it before he spoke. A moment later he had gained his control. He said in a flat, taut tone, 'Virginia, what *did* my mother tell you? Look, that's over long since. It was a flash-in-the-pan affair, most unsuitable, and Melanie knew it. She couldn't possibly have faced this sort of life, and that's all there is to it. We're here.'

There was a white school-house, with actually a couple of ponies tethered under the trees, a store, a garage, a white wooden church with a green tower and a shining slender steeple, and a modern public hall. It was at a cross-roads. Leicester, determined to bring this conversation back to a degree of normality, said, pointing up one of the roads, that sloped upwards, 'The Manse is round the next bend, you can't see it for the trees. You'll love it. When we're married, Virginia, we'll get up early and go mushrooming up that hill.'

It sounded idyllic. But would it be? Leicester stopped at the store where a bus was standing. 'I'll just collect the mail.' He went into the store, head up, confident, smiling. And well he might be ... he'd had most of it his way so far. She looked up at the bus, and saw that the destination sign said: 'Oamaru.'

She was out of the car on the instant and around at the boot. Thank goodness most of her stuff was being sent on, so she was taking only her new things. She grabbed her case and the rug and walked over to the bus driver and handed them to him. There were plenty of spare seats. He stowed them in the luggage compartment at the side.

'When do you leave?' she asked breathlessly, one apprehensive eye on the door of the store. Oh, please let him get delayed with a garrulous parishioner, or have him have to wait in a queue for his letters, oh, let something, anything hold him up! I mustn't stay. It isn't going to work.

I've got to get away to think things out for myself.

The bus driver said nonchalantly, 'We leave in about sixty seconds, lady.' He handed her in. Sure was a looker, this girl. She'd just come in with the padre. Wonder who she is?

Virginia was just getting her change back from the driver, standing beside him, when Leicester reached the step. Her eyes dared him to make a fuss, though it was scarcely likely with half his parish looking on.

'Thank you for the lift, Mr. Gordon,' she said, for their benefit and to save his face, 'and good-bye.' The bus moved off.

She ought to have felt triumph at thus outwitting him; she ought to have felt pleased she had not given in too quickly, but she didn't.

She was desolately recalling the way he had said 'Melanie.' Never had he ever said 'Virginia' quite like that. She had a conviction that somewhere along the line both she and Leicester had taken a wrong turning.

In Oamaru Virginia made some inquiries, then went to the Post Office to ring her mother. She recounted her adventures.

'So I'm taking another bus later this afternoon, but just to Timaru. Leicester is wild enough to dash up to Christchurch to the Clarendon – unfortunately I told him where I'd be staying – and honestly, Mother, I feel I must get away from everybody and solve that problem myself. He could only do it tonight, because he's got a meeting to-morrow-night and a very busy week after that, naturally, with his week-end coming up. I'll go on to Christchurch tomorrow. I'll ring the Clarendon and cancel tonight's room.'

Mrs. Fergusson said approvingly, 'Good for you, darling. There were times when I'd like to have put a bomb under you – the way you took Leicester's casual treatment. Even your father noticed it. Perhaps he *is* the one for you – I don't know – only you can decide that, but it won't do him any harm to have to exert himself.'

Virginia said, 'And Mother, when I get a flat, don't tell Leicester the address – he'll come up between Sundays if you do, and it will not only interfere with my writing, it will unsettle me. If he rings to ask for it, just tell him to write home and you'll forward the letters on. I must have time to think.'

After Virginia had hung up on what had been a costly call, Mrs. Fergusson went in search of her husband, shaking with laughter. What fun for Virginia!

Three days later Virginia was sitting on a seat in the shadow of Captain Scott's statue, so lovingly sculptured by his wife, for this city whence the famous explorer had sailed on his last voyage.

She was idly throwing bread to the ducks on the gentle Avon, and to the gulls on the grass who made this favourite lunch-hour spot for the city's workers a happy hunting-ground for titbits, when someone came to sit on the seat beside her.

Virginia glanced up. 'Why, Mrs. Morgan!' she exclaimed with delight. The woman's pleasure matched her own.

Virginia said: 'I didn't know you were back in New Zealand, even.'

Mrs. Morgan was an old college friend of her mother's and one of New Zealand's foremost artists. She had a gift of friendship for the young. Two years ago she had gone on a long visit to Britain, following the death of her husband.

'I'm settling in Christchurch now,' said Gwyneth Morgan, 'this is my birthplace, you know, though I lived in about nine places after I married. Now Kenneth is settled here I'd like to be near him – though not too near. Mary, his wife, and I are the best of friends, in fact I think you could say kindred spirits, and I know we'll remain that way as long as we both have homes of our own. When you're the mother of an only son you have to guard against becoming possessive.

'I like to be near enough to go over to baby-sit for them if they want to get out together, so I've bought a house in Avonside near Linwood Avenue. They live in Shirley, that's why I came to sit here for a bit. I'm tired out tramping round auction rooms for the extra furniture I need. This house is very large – ridiculous really for one woman – and it needs massive furniture. Besides modern stuff doesn't suit me. I kept a fair bit after Francis died, but not too much, because I had to store it and I'd never dreamed I'd take on a place so big. And, Virginia' – she looked a trifle shamefaced for a moment as though confessing a serious fault – 'I bought it for sheer sentiment's sake.'

Virginia looked interested. Gwyneth Morgan continued: 'My father and I often used to walk round Avonside when I was a girl and Father always used to say it reminded him of the sort that American author, Grace S. Richmond, used to write about. When I was twenty I painted it for him. I still have it. It's a funny old house, but I love it.'

In ten minutes they were off in a taxi to see it. Virginia stood with her hand on the gate, taking it in. It was quaint rather than an architectural masterpiece, but it had an air. Squarish and tall, it had verandahs on both storeys and at one side a sort of annexe, evidently added at a much later date. This had diamond-paned French windows opening on to a small front porch and it was latticed to hold climbing roses.

The garden was weedy, but standard roses were blooming, and Michaelmas daisies and low box borders that could soon be clipped to orthodox neatness edged the asphalt paths.

They came to an iron fountain, a rather charmingly grotesque one, that made tinkling music as the water fell, blending with the soft lap-lap of the Avon flowing at the far side of the road.

Gwyneth led the way inside. It was still cluttered up with packing-cases and straw, yet somehow even so bore the unmistakable stamp of Gwyneth Morgan's personality, Gwyneth Morgan, artist.

They were having a cup of tea in the kitchen before Gwyneth realized that Virginia was not in Christchurch on holiday, but here to stay and looking for a flat or rooms.

'I've been so busy talking over my own plans and being schoolgirlishly enthusiastic over them, I've not given you a chance. Virginia, how providential – I mean you looking for somewhere to write. Kenneth hates me being in this great place all alone, and that annexe is really a small flat – it's got its own kitchenette and bathroom – but I decided not to let it as there's so little chance of getting a really kindred spirit in. The room that has the best lighting for a studio overlooks the sitting-room of the annexe and I like to work at all sorts of odd hours. Sounds frightfully selfish of me, but I didn't want squalling babies down below or young ones making the air hideous with pop music when I need to concentrate – but you'd want quiet too – no, I'd never notice a typewriter going – that's rhythmic. Oh, do say you'll come!'

She took a key from a hook. 'Come and see it. There's a way in from here, of course, but the proper way is to view it from the front.'

Virginia couldn't believe her incredible luck. She thought of some of the rooms she had looked at yesterday . . . those within her means had been dark, some damp, most of them quite ugly and depressing. They had all been furnished. But Gwyneth was asking so little for this, she'd gladly furnish it herself.

Here, the French windows led into a sitting-room that faced north, so got the sun there almost all day, and there was a double casement window set in the west wall where Virginia creeper peeped in and would be a splendid place for watching sunsets. It had a padded window-seat. There was a dining alcove with a built-in table and seats – a great saving in furnishing.

The woodwork was painted a sort of stone colour and the fireplace was brick and wide. The bedroom looked down the garden path at the back where an old gnarled grapevine twined lovingly roung a broken-down rustic arbour and appeared to be holding it up. Poplars and cypresses shut off the sight of the other houses and it had a privacy that Virginia knew would be a great incentive to work.

Bathroom and kitchenette proved to be minute cubicles contrived out of one small room, but were adequate.

'I could certainly work in this room,' said Virginia, returning to the sitting-room and visualizing her typewriter under the west window, the Avon purling along musically, the scents sweeping in from the garden throughout the changing seasons. With a shock she realized she was already picturing herself as staying here permanently. Good ... that meant she had stopped mentally planning a future with Leicester.

Gwyneth said, 'I must confess I've felt a little lonely at nights, but with you tapping away down here, I'd feel I had company. Why not stay with me tonight, I've got a spare bed?'

Virginia departed in a taxi to pack her things. Gwyneth was considerably surprised when, two hours later, a truck drove up to the door, and furniture began to be unloaded. Before she could reach the gate, Virginia emerged from a taxi behind it.

'I went to a secondhand shop and bought some stuff. Not much – just the bare necessities. Dad gave me a very generous cheque, so I was really thrilled I hadn't spent much of it. I got a new mattress and pillow and blankets and linen, but the rest is all secondhand.'

There was a bed and a chest of drawers, an easy chair, a carpet, a little worn, but with a good floral pattern, dimmed by time into a harmonious blend of rose and grey and lavender, and a long, narrow table with two drawers at one end.

'What on earth is that very odd-looking piece of furniture? It looks as if it's been made out of an old washstand.'

Virginia grinned. 'A makeshift desk. I'll have my own sent up from home, but it will take time, and this would be very useful in other ways, I'm sure.' She regarded it with affection, as one might a mongrel dog. 'It's long enough to take a typewriter at one end and a pile of exercise books at the other. I know I could have written at the dining-room table, but I can't bear having to clear things off when I'm working.'

There were bookcases each side of the old-fashioned fireplace and Gwyneth said there was plenty of firing in the shed at the back left by the previous tenant. Virginia felt her career had really begun.

Gwyneth started to chuckle. 'I didn't think you were so impetuous, Virginia. But I like it. I used to feel you were vivid to look at but—' she came to a confused full stop.

'But rather dull,' finished Virginia, entirely without rancour. She remembered her mother recounting some of the scrapes Gwyneth Morgan's unthinking candour had led her into in their college days. Gwyneth always started to say exactly what she was thinking, even if prudence sometimes caught up with her before she finished.

'Well, not exactly dull, but not as interesting as you should have been. You were too – too – oh, what's the word I want? – too conformable. Didn't kick over the traces enough.'

Virginia nodded. 'I did mentally – when I first had to go into drapery. I just hated it. But I've always had an outlet in my writing. I used to let myself go in my journals. I'm a bit ashamed of all I wrote in them, now. But it was a safety valve until I got rid of the sort of intellectual snobbery I'd unwittingly developed. And till I came to appreciate the real worth of the people I was working with.

'But now it must be my red hair coming into its own, plus a certain freedom I'll know in this city. One needs to be – sort of circumspect when a daughter of the manse. Here I'm going to be nobody but myself . . . Virginia Jane Fergusson . . . author of one obscure and as yet unpublished book called *Up and at 'em*.'

'Not really? – Well, I mean I know you told me you'd had a book accepted, but is that really the name? Sounds like a clan-call or something. Oh, that's an idea. Is it the

57

clan-call of the Fergussons?'

Virginia laughed. 'No, their motto is "Sweeter after difficulties." '

Gwyneth looked thoughtful. 'That's what this experience you're passing through may very well prove. No, don't mistake me, I don't mean that it will necessarily bring you and Leicester to a happy ending. It just may, if you're right for each other, but from what you've told me, it may very well be that you haven't met the right one yet, Virginia.'

'Meanwhile,' said Virginia, 'I'm tired of emotion, and all I want to do is lay this carpet and get on with some typing!'

But before she settled to that she had dinner with Gwyneth, then rang her mother. That call cost Virginia four dollars but was well worth it.

'There's quite a bit of mail here for you, darling,' said her mother. 'Penny, go and fetch Virginia's mail from the hall table. Let me see ... they're all typewritten ... one from Auckland, two from Australia, one from England.'

'Fat or thin?' demanded Virginia quickly.

'All thin.'

'Good. They sound like acceptances. Would you like to rip them open and just tell me briefly what they are.'

Virginia felt that that mail had set the seal upon her venture. Two well-paid short stories from Australia, the same for a poem in an English magazine, and the Auckland one was from a newspaper editor. He had liked the sample series of column work Virginia had sent him almost a month ago. He would like two a week for at least three months. It could become a permanent assignment if it proved a popular column and she could keep the standard up. He would take ten of the samples, and would return her the other two with suggestions for coopering them more to the needs of his paper. He mentioned a price.

'How absolutely marvellous,' said Virginia. 'That will pay my rent and a bit over. Now I've only got to earn my provisions. And clothes when I need them, but thanks to you and Dad, I shan't need any for ages.'

Virginia felt as if the seal of success was upon her venture.

A week later she was well settled in. Her own personal belongings had come up from Dunedin, pictures and vases and ornaments, and, of course, a case of books. There was also much stuff her mother deemed essential for her comfort, and the flat was now a home. This, thought Virginia, was the life for her!

Instead of spending the inspirational morning hours on concocting things like: 'New and natty ... natural deerskin bags, cane handles, chromium fittings, steel-studded at base,' etc., etc., she could spend her mornings with her fictional characters, living with them, rejoicing, sorrowing, triumphing. She felt her dialogue took on a new sparkle, her descriptions more colour, her emotions more depth. And she was gloriously free, unhampered by thoughts of what Mrs. Gordon might think, when they appeared in print.

Nevertheless, there was one thing missing and she became more and more aware of it ... the stimulation of more numerous human contacts than those provided by Gwyneth and her friends.

Virginia now knew full well the value of those years among a big staff at Warrington's, the dozens of conflicting natures and problems, the fun and variety they had enjoyed. Virginia had loved working with them.

Not at first, of course. She had to admit that. But after she had lost her natural frustration at the interrupting of her chosen career, she had admitted to herself, as a new set of values widened and deepened, that if she hadn't come here she might never have gained the warm human touch that now characterized her written work.

She had gone home and underlined a clipping in her journal, kept because it interested her, though hadn't meant as much to her till now. Faith Baldwin had said it: 'I am inclined to believe that the closer the artist is brought to the common facts of humanity, the finer the art.'

Virginia sat at her desk, chin in hand, gazing at the wall

59

in front of her. She'd been like this for an hour What was wrong with her? Perhaps she had *too* much time. Perhaps it was true that when you were pressed for it, you had the goad of being determined to wrest from the busy hours time for what you loved most? Yet she had sought inspiration. She had soaked herself in Christchurch pioneer history and had reaped the benefit in articles for the *Star*. She had visited the museum and revelled in its beauty and interest; she had explored every leafy lane, the beautiful Cathedral, centred in the very heart of the city, the old Provincial Chambers, rich in history, and all the byways.

She donned her Robin Hood green suit and began to walk towards the city. Her steps led her almost unaware to the world she knew. How strange that in this lovely city with its many churches, its cloistered and ivied courts of learning, she instinctively, when in need of inspiration, sought the commercial world.

She turned into the first draper's she saw. Fenton's was not the largest in the city by any means, but it had a spaciousness and charm that appealed to her. Potted shrubs and flowers seemed used largely in decor, the carpets were deep and muffling, and the lighting was excellent. The draping displays were done by a master hand. Virginia's trained eye took all this in. Suddenly she itched to describe these things. How too ridiculous! This was what she had run from.

To get her mind off it, she decided to try on hats. She had only the one with her, and though most of the time she scorned wearing them, there were occasions when you had to don one.

She instantly saw the very thing. In bronze with a tiny splash of this same green and, lying temptingly beside it, a pigskin bag with a diagonal inset of the bronze and green. She didn't need the bag, but—

A salesgirl came forward and took Virginia and the hat to a table with a mirror. She had decided on the hat and was still trying to resist the bag, when she heard voices from a door ajar nearby. The man's voice was deep and slightly drawling.

'This is the only part of the business that drives me mad,' it said. 'I can imagine an effect with a window and describe it to the window-dressers till they too see it and produce it. I can go on a buying spree and order stuff to the tune of thousands and remain confident in my own judgment ... but this advertising stunt drives me mad. I've read everything on the subject you can imagine – I study magazines from London to Los Angeles, but never a really original idea do I get. That's why Latham's ads attract customers more than ours do – oh, I'm positive about that, Mrs. Chester. And it's the young grandson who does it. He has a flair for it. If they never used a single illustration in their full-page ads, they could sell the things from his descriptions alone. You need someone with a gift with words. How the devil am I going to describe this creation, Mrs. Chester?'

And the speaker emerged into the millinery showroom, twirling a jaunty and expensive copper model on a finger. He stopped and regarded it with loathing.

Before she could stop herself Virginia had spoken. 'I'll describe it for you, if you like.'

Had Virginia been pale and dowdy and mouse-coloured, no doubt the debonair manager of Fenton's would have icily begged her pardon and swept on, but the wing of burnished hair under the green hat was arresting to say the least; and the eyes, that in this light, were sparklingly green.

'I used to be in the advertising department at Warrington's in Dunedin – in fact in charge of it,' said Virginia calmly, and just as calmly relieved him of his ball-point and pad. She narrowed her eyes to look at the hat still wobbling on his finger, twitched it round, then scribbled madly.

'How's this?' She read: 'It has been said, and said truly, that a woman views life from a new angle when she wears a new hat, and undoubtedly this hat has the newest and most daring of angles.

'Contrived with genius and styled by Jeremy Pearce, in copper-bronze fur felt, this may be seen in Fenton's millinery salon, priced at twelve dollars.'

The manager looked at her. 'And I spent half last night thinking about the new hats. Result nothing!'

He hesitated, then said, 'You said you *used* to work for Warrington's. Have you taken a post somewhere else – I mean are you in Christchurch just on holiday? Or—' his eyes travelled to her left hand but couldn't see it properly, 'are you married now and not wanting a job?'

'N-no – I'm not. At least I mean I'm not married, but I don't—'

'Would you come into my office and talk?'

Virginia turned to the salesgirl. 'Would you put that hat and bag to one side? I'll pay for it in a few moments.'

'My name's Muir,' said the manager as he closed the door of his office. 'And yours?'

'Virginia Fergusson. But I'm not looking for a position.'

Mr. Muir groaned. 'I thought not. It sounded too good to be true. If we could get the services of the one who's been responsible for Warrington's adverts these last few years it would be ideal. Why don't you want a position?'

Virginia explained that she was attempting to make her living solely by free-lance journalism now.

'H'mm. Well, if that's the situation, I suppose we can't expect you to change your mind just because Fenton's desperately need an advertising clerk!'

Virginia said: 'I've tried for years to do it in the evenings – only I don't feel you do your best work then. You're usually sort of mentally spent with all the doings of the day. I wanted morning hours, particularly.'

A gleam shot into the manager's eyes. 'How about parttime? I can handle bread-and-butter stuff, sale bargains and so on – but the super stuff for the weeklies and periodicals stumps me.'

Virginia sat up erectly, betraying interest. Ever since she had set up her desk at Mrs. Morgan's house she had had qualms. Free-lancing was patchy. When you didn't depend on it, every success was a delightful surprise and an extra.

When you did, you were aware of an inner anxiety and tenseness, which did nothing at all for your work.

Mr. Muir said quickly, 'How about four afternoons a week? I'm afraid you'd have to start about eleven-thirty – because of newspaper deadlines – and have one to two dinner-hour, but if it were only Tuesday to Friday, could you manage that? I mean we work Friday night till nine, same as all the other shops, and you could do Monday stuff then. I take it you wouldn't object to Friday nights? If you could we'd offer you—'

And to Virginia's hastily concealed surprise he offered exactly what she had been getting at Warrington's. Laughter bubbled within her, carefully repressed. Did, or really didn't, it pay to revolt?

The same salary, her Mondays free, which meant three days for writing, apart from church-going, and a flat of her own. A thousand blessings on Les Warrington and Leicester's mother, who had triggered this off for her!

That reminded her. Oh dear. Naturally she hadn't needed a reference. But no doubt this man would ask for one. She frowned and took a quick look at Mr. Muir.

He had the crowsfeet lines that humour etches at the corners of the eyes and a good-tempered mouth, and, in spite of an over-elegant appearance that suggested too much the air of a man about town for Virginia's taste, he looked understanding.

Of course drapers were prone to be too sartorially perfect, so she need not hold that against him.

She plunged. 'I think I should tell you why I left Warrington's.' (There was no need, of course, to bring Leicester into it.)

When she had finished, Mr. Muir said gravely and with a real poker face, 'Thank you for telling me. I imagine it wasn't easy. Sort of thing that happens out of the blue. I'm glad, for Fenton's sake, it did. I've met Martha Warrington – she has the reputation for being extremely eccentric. Can you start next Tuesday? Is there anything you'll

63

want to know? We'll give you the salary mentioned – and a little office of your own – and—' his brown eyes twinkled, '. . . no one will kiss you.'

Virginia was annoyed to find herself blushing hotly.

She wasn't to know that Mr. Muir had been noting the almost iridescent green of her eyes under the bronze eyebrows, the curve of her lips and her throat, and deciding he for one didn't blame young Warrington!

Virginia, to cover her embarrassment, said quickly, 'I must go back to the millinery department and fix up for the bag and hat.'

'Oh, yes, just a moment.' Mr. Muir scribbled something on a memo pad and handed it to her. 'Give that to the assistant – to let her know that you're now entitled to ten per cent staff discount.'

Virginia took a taxi home out of sheer exuberance of spirit and decided she might, after all, answer the last letter her mother had forwarded from home from Leicester.

It had been a fine letter, full of whimsicalities and feeling – Virginia hadn't been able to resist feeling a traitorous warmth towards him when she had first read it, but then had reminded herself that for some reason, Leicester had always sounded more ardent on paper than he was in the flesh. And his postscript had made her mad. It had said: 'And don't forget, darling, if the free-lancing doesn't pay, the Manse and I are waiting!'

Virginia had gritted her teeth and said: 'I'm *going* to make a success of it, so there!'

Yes, she'd write tonight – after all, it was five days old – and casually mention that she had a part-time job for the same salary as before, a contract for newspaper articles, and she had sold two short stories in Australia this week.

CHAPTER FOUR

It worked out well. The new job proved stimulating and Virginia felt she had a standing at Fenton's that she had never had at Warrington's, where she had had to work her way up. It often turned out like that. You made your way, then took a better position, somewhere where no one could remember you as a junior.

Mr. Muir hardly ever altered a word she wrote, and as Virginia did not trade on this – indeed it made her more than ever conscientious about her work – things went really well.

She had been a little perturbed when she first found out that Fenton's was owned by Mrs. Terence Fenton, who had been in Auckland on a buying expedition when she was engaged. She'd rather it had been run by a company. She'd had enough of family businesses, she felt.

She said to Mr. Muir, 'I felt after my experience at Warrington's I'd rather not work for a woman again – fond and all as I am of my own sex. They make things too personal. A man regards one more as a cog in the machine and that's all I want to be. But perhaps Mrs. Fenton is different.'

Mr. Muir said: 'She's a fine woman who has known a lot of sadness in her life. I'll admit there are times when she exasperates me, but I so admire her grit. So will you when you get to know her. Besides, you have no need to worry ... *she* hasn't got a susceptible son!'

Virginia looked at him reproachfully. 'Forget that, would you? I only told you because I had to tell you why I left.'

He grinned. 'Actually Mrs. Fenton would make a good copy. Better study her.'

Virginia sighed. 'I have so much imagination I don't need to study people and use them – they pop into my mind endowed with character and fully clothed!'

Mr. Muir did not tell her that it was contrary to custom to engage staff without Mrs. Fenton's approval. But she admitted that in this case, it had been necessary to snap Virginia up. The business now warranted an advertising clerk.

Mrs. Fenton was out at dinner – she took twelve to one – and Mr. Muir was finishing the orders of some Australian samples, the costing-clerk taking them down in triplicate.

'It's just on one, Miss Marshall. You can go now and I'll get away too.'

He came out of Mrs. Fenton's office and into his own and put the samples on to his desk. The door into Virginia's office was open a little.

He heard her voice: 'No, Leicester, thank you. I really *have* got an appointment.' Her tone was cool and positive and carried no note of regret. 'I *can't* lunch with you.'

Then a man's voice, rather a charming one. 'Don't be absurd, darling. It's not every day you get me in Christchurch. Ring up and put it off.'

'I haven't any intention of putting it off, Leicester.'

'It's the hairdresser, I suppose – though your hair looks charming to me. You simply couldn't improve on it at the moment. Ring her up, my love, and say your young man's come to town. She'll forgive you. All women are romantic. She'll feel she's assisting a romance to blossom and will say: "Go with my blessing, child".'

Virginia was unmoved. In fact she snorted. 'It's not the hairdresser, and the person I have the appointment with would be far from interested in furthering the romance – yours or anyone's. Do I make myself clear that I am *not* lunching with you?'

Mr. Muir thought the fellow mighty persistent. She'd called him Lester. It must be young Warrington. Les. Mr. Muir's mouth twitched; darned if he wouldn't lend a hand!

He pushed the door open just a fraction more as if he had no idea anyone else save Virginia was in the office. 'Virginia,' he said, 'hurry up and get your bonnet on, there's

66

a dear. If we leave it too late all the best tables at Shaw's will be gone again. I forgot to order one.'

For one startled moment Virginia's face would have given her away had Leicester been looking, but he was trying to see who was behind that door.

Virginia dropped her lashes swiftly to hide her mirth as Mr. Muir deliberately came into full view and gave a well-simulated start. 'Oh, sorry, Miss Fergusson, I didn't realize you had – er – a pressman, is it? – here.' He backed into his office again, adding, 'But don't be long, will you?'

Virginia didn't have a 'bonnet', but she slipped off her office smock, took down her jacket and donned it quickly. She'd renewed her make-up just ten minutes ago.

'You will excuse us, won't you?' she said to Leicester, as Mr. Muir reappeared, hat in hand.

He put a possessive hand under her elbow and whisked her out of the door.

His car was right outside the staff entrance as a mechanic had brought it there not five minutes ago. There was no chance of any conversation as he swung into the busy dinner-hour traffic.

Shaw's was an emporium with its own customer car-park. Mr. Muir was wasting no time. He had her out of the car and directly into the restaurant from the lobby in a few quick movements, it seemed to Virginia. She was installed in a corner seat by the head waiter before she had time to get her breath and collect her wits.

She leaned forward in her seat and said to Mr. Muir, looking at him searchingly, 'Perhaps you would explain?'

Mr. Muir shook out his napkin and smiled. 'Did it well, didn't I? Sheer inspiration of the moment. I feel quite the knight-errant. As soon as I heard you prosing on about your appointment, I realized who it was and thought I'd do my daily good deed – I used to be a Boy Scout, you know – and rescue you from young Warrington.'

Virginia looked blank, then digested this for a moment in silence. 'Young Warrington? It wasn't Les Warrington! It was Leicester Gordon, the Reverend Leicester Gordon.

In fact, till I came up here I was practically engaged to him.'

The consternation on the face of the usually suave and imperturbable manager was almost too much for Virginia. She gazed hastily out of the window and tried not to giggle.

'Holy mackerel!' he said. 'Will he take an explanation? Perhaps I should be the one to make it. I mean – oh, I say, he does know about young Warrington and why you left, does he? Oh, lord, if he doesn't – well, the fat will be in the fire with a vengeance.' He groaned.

Virginia sobered up and said breathlessly, 'Look, it doesn't matter a bit. The near-engagement is off, anyway. And after all, I *was* refusing him. It's only natural you thought what you did, and uncommonly decent of you to rush into the fray. I was being purposely vague about the appointment to annoy him and what you did gave it some strong local colour. It's a frightfully long story, but I think I'll have to tell you – in part, anyway. You seem doomed to listen to my affairs.'

Mr. Muir grinned. 'Well, let's have it, but here's the waitress coming. Are you going to have soup or fruit juice?'

'Soup – *toheroa*. But first I'll have to ring my dentist! Do you think they'd let me use that phone at the cash-desk?'

Mr. Muir groaned. 'Haven't I put my foot in it? You'll have to say the manager of the firm – an irascible fellow – detained you and you couldn't get away. Look, on second thoughts I'll call the dentist for you and explain that I detained you. Which one?'

'Dr. Farquhar Steele. It's my first visit to him.'

His brow cleared. 'Rufe Steele is a friend of mine – as well as my own dentist. I play golf with him. I'll fix it.'

He was back in a few moments and they began their soup. The manager grinned, 'Yesterday I made a vow never to come back here again – but in the excitement of the moment I clean forgot.'

Virginia looked curious. 'What happened? Slug in the lettuce?'

'No, I must have lapsed into a day-dream while waiting

for the sweet. I suddenly realized that the fellow at the next table had been waiting an age without having his order taken, and before I knew what I was doing, I'd sung out: "Forward one!" at the top of my voice, just as if it was our own showroom. Certainly he got attended to at top speed, but you should have seen the look the waitress gave me, to say nothing of the chap and all the other diners! I swallowed my sweet in about two gulps and didn't wait for coffee.'

Virginia laughed heartily with him and began to view her impeccable manager with new eyes. He was younger than she had thought at first, anyway.

They got to the coffee stage. Mr. Muir grinned at her and said, 'After all that's happened, you can't possibly go on calling me Mr. Muir. Make it Nicholas.'

Virginia said, 'Well, for this dinner-hour only. But at two o'clock of course, it's back to Mr. Muir.'

Nicholas Muir looked up as someone paused at their table, someone who was as redheaded as Virginia. A peculiar look crossed the manager's face, though the look on the stranger's face was one of unadulterated glee.

Mr. Muir said, to Virginia's consternation, 'Good lord, Rufe!' and Farquhar Steele said, 'Don't think a thing about it. I don't blame you one scrap for detaining your advertising clerk for so long . . . and in so pleasant a fashion. And I told you I could use the time.' He grinned, 'I take it this *is* the clerk . . . and my client?'

Mr. Muir gulped and made the necessary introduction. 'It's a good story, Rufe. I'll tell it to you some time. Meanwhile, we're just going. This table suit you?'

It did. Virginia was glad to get away. When they got outside they looked at each other and said a heartfelt: 'Phew!'

'I've got to pick up a book I've ordered at a little shop in Cashel Street. Quaint sort of place. Just your style, I'd say.'

'Thank you,' said Virginia, hugely enjoying herself, 'that's a fine compliment. I never thought of myself as quaint before!'

'This is just not my day,' said Mr. Muir.

The bookshop was rather dim and altogether delightful. In the far corner was an Indian rug and a couple of good chairs on it. Bookshelves jutting out gave it an air of seclusion and positively induced one to browse. There was a small round table with some copies of *Punch* and a couple of good paintings on the walls above the bookshelves. One was a still-life study and the other an interior, a simple study . . . the curve of a staircase, a row of books, a gleam of brass on a window on the landing, and the only strong light in it came from an open casement. To redeem the inanimate look some interiors possess, there was a rug awry on the polished floor as if only lately someone had flung across the hall and rushed upstairs. It needed only a glance at it to tell Virginia this was one of Gwyneth Morgan's.

Nicholas put Virginia into one of the chairs. 'I want to see the old chap who runs this. Rum old cove but very interesting. Take a good look at him. He's so delightfully typical . . . like something out of Dickens. Always wears a smoking-cap, a black velvet affair with a puce tassel. Shouldn't be at all surprised if he wears a night-shirt too.'

'But in bed,' suggested Virginia.

He grinned. 'Like something to read? The old man's as slow as a snail.'

She shook her head. 'No, I'll just absorb atmosphere.'

But she didn't. Unobserved by him, she watched Nicholas Muir.

He was standing at the counter, tall and well turned out, playing with a little brass bell he had just tinkled. Everything he wore was perfectly toned. He was dark, with a sort of brooding look. An interesting personality.

She thought of what she had heard the costing clerk, Alison Marshall, say of him to another new girl: 'Steer clear of Nicholas Muir. He's not the marrying sort – a perfect bachelor. Has a flat in Bryndwyr, I believe. Looks after himself in the main, I've heard. I can well imagine he doesn't want a resident housekeeper. Might curb his entertaining!'

She had laughed and Virginia had hated the sly, meaning sound of it, but since the remarks were not addressed to her, she could say nothing. 'A very gay dog,' Alison had added.

But now Virginia could only think that sophistication had a certain charm, heady but exciting.

For the first time Virginia wondered what had happened to Leicester.

Nicholas Muir sauntered over to her, two books under his arm. He offered her one. 'Would you accept this, to mark an occasion?'

'Thank you,' said Virginia, then 'thank you' again, much more warmly, when she saw it was poetry.

Nicholas Muir twinkled at her. 'You may find some of it rather strong meat, and not all of it's good, but some of it's unbelievably beautiful. It's worth sifting out the gold from the dross.'

Virginia dimpled, 'I rather believe I'm in the mood for strong meat. I seem to have got the bit between my teeth.'

'These redheaded women!' drawled Nicholas Muir. 'I believe they're supposed to be very exciting. And in spite of my reputation, I've never dallied with a redhead.'

Leicester was waiting outside for her when closing time came. Virginia got demurely into his car. They measured glances.

'I've got seats for the Regent tonight, and no jiggery-pokery about coming. No previous engagements. Where would you like to go for tea?'

'We can go to my place,' said Virginia, much to his surprise. 'Go round the river – Oxford Terrace side, not Cambridge – about a couple of miles, going east.'

The sun was westering and the river was like a stream of reflected molten gold between the spans of the bridges. A gentle breeze flaked the leaves from the Lombardy poplars that lined the banks and kept them floating in the air like snowflakes arrested in falling. 'Isn't Christchurch beautiful?' cried Virginia, in the tone of one who has found her lodestar.

'Yes,' said Leicester, with a notable lack of enthusiasm. But he thawed out when he reached the flat. He was shown Gwyneth's studio while Virginia made the tea. Gwyneth herself had proposed this, wanting to look him over.

By the time Leicester had disposed of a featherweight omelette with herbs and gherkins, and tinned pears and cream, he had mellowed considerably.

Virginia brought coffee, with a plate of the cheese wafers he was very fond of, and set them out on a small table she had bought, near the fire.

'You like a bit of whipped cream on top, don't you, Leicester?'

'I do – but one thing I don't like, and that's you so far away.'

He put her into the easy chair and sat on the arm of it, and waited upon her. Then he removed the cups and pushed the table away. He put a finger under her chin. 'And now, Madam Mischief, please explain. Who's the fellow you went to lunch with?'

'Nicholas Muir,' said Virginia lightly. 'That's why I couldn't break the appointment. He's the manager.'

Leicester made an impatient gesture. 'You aren't going to pretend it's policy when asked to dine out with the management? Not you – after all, you didn't hesitate to brush Les Warrington off.'

'Oh, it wasn't policy. Whatever made you think that? It was sheer pleasure. Les was a rattle-pate. Nicholas Muir is a very different kettle of fish – an interesting man, very complex, quite fascinating.'

'Oh, come off it, Jinny – I mean Virginia. Stop talking as if you were analysing one of your own fictional characters. Are you really attracted by this chap?'

Virginia considered it thoughtfully and obviously. 'We-ll, y-es,' she finally admitted. 'Yes, I'd say he was definitely a charmer. But what does it matter? I've said I'll go out with you tonight.'

Leicester leaned over and took her in his arms. 'Virginia,

72

you're a little wretch! You're doing this to pay me out for being too casual earlier!'

'Well, it started that way,' she admitted, 'but I'm finding it so enjoyable to shop around a bit! I'd got into a rut.'

Mmm. Leicester had come to life. When had he ever kissed her like this? An unwelcome thought struck her. Had his feeling for Melanie been like this? She pushed it away from her.

'Where are you staying tonight, Leicester?'

'Oh, I thought of ringing up a chap I was at Knox College with. He's got a manse in a new housing area here. I'll have to look him up in the phone book. Has Gwyneth got the phone on?'

Virginia relented a little. 'Actually, I think she would put you up.' She would, and did.

Leicester did feel she was softening a little. He thoroughly enjoyed the rest of the evening, except when, at supper-time, and they had not long been in, Nicholas Muir rang up. He couldn't make much of the conversation, because it was through the door into Gwyneth's hall. He just heard her say: 'Oh, yes, Nicholas, it was a fine picture. A good English cast. You ought to see it if you haven't yet. Well, thanks for ringing. Goodbye, Nicholas, see you tomorrow.'

Leicester had fidgeted while she was speaking and listening and picked up a new book lying on top of the bookcase. There on the flyleaf in bold black, characterful writing was: 'Memento of a happy mistake . . . Nicholas Muir to Virginia.'

Now what the devil did that mean? He might ruin the evening by asking; better not press his luck too far.

Altogether when Leicester left the next morning, he felt the visit had been only moderately worth while. He had not before seen Virginia so delightfully dressed, so confident, so blithe, so – confoundedly distant.

She kissed him goodbye with a sort of tongue-in-the-cheek air. He found himself wondering if that fellow Muir had kissed her yet. Blast him . . . and Greenhaughs was a good hundred and seventy miles away. What had got into

73

his once placid Jinny, anyway?

It was a fortnight later and Virginia was sitting at her desk yawning. It had been a slow day. She'd much rather be busy. She was feeling bored and disgruntled, and she wasn't used to such emotions.

Nothing pleasant or exciting had happened of late ... or was it just that after so much turmoil and unexpected happenings, it was inevitable there should be a reaction?

After that first encouraging spate of acceptances there had been nothing in the mail for her for days except fat rejections. Nothing was right. Her typewriter had developed a kink in its innards and in the very first of a short series of articles she had had accepted by a Christchurch newspaper there was a misprint so ambiguous, misleading and comical that she had positively squirmed!

Why must everything go wrong at once? Not for anything would Virginia admit to herself that the shop life at Fenton's was horribly flat with Nicholas Muir away. He had been in Dunedin almost a week on a business trip.

Still, she had come to know Sarah Fenton better with him away. It had meant closer contact. But she was aware that Alison Marshall hadn't liked that. The costing-clerk positively fawned on Sarah Fenton, and didn't like anyone else being too friendly with her. Virginia hated petty jealousy.

She finished up measuring a block of ads, thumbed over a page of notes and substituted 'severely classical lines' for 'austerely tailored effects' and wondered what difference she thought she had made.

Well, her day was nearly over. The house telephone rang – Sarah Fenton requesting her presence in her own office.

As a rule Mrs. Fenton was extremely self-possessed. She had clear, cameo-like features and smooth black hair and most natural and artistic faint shadows round her darkly blue eyes.

But now she seemed very vague and it was a trivial matter to discuss right on closing-time. The discussion, such as it

74

was, came to an end and Sarah, of all things, went on to discuss the weather. She got almost garrulous about it. Then all of a sudden she made up her mind.

'Miss Fergusson, there's something I feel I must say to you. I'm a woman a lot older than you – and I feel I should. Please don't be offended. It's just that – well, I don't feel it's at all wise for a girl to let any attentions the manager may pay her go to her head.'

Virginia stared. Then she remembered that Alison Marshall had seen her come back from lunch with Mr. Muir that day.

Mrs. Fenton said, 'You see, it's awkward for the poor man, working with such a large crowd of girls and being a bachelor, especially such an eligible one. We – he and I – both agree that business – well, that business should be kept strictly apart from anything else.' She looked at Virginia. 'I don't need to say anything more, do I?'

Virginia got up, and her voice was quite tense. 'No, you don't need to say anything more, Mrs. Fenton.'

Mrs. Fenton knew a moment of panic. This girl was going to give in her notice. She said quickly, 'You – you need not say to Mr. Muir, of course, that I've said this – just that if he asks you out again, I should find an excuse if I were you.'

Virginia smiled faintly. 'Thank you for the advice, Mrs. Fenton. No, I'll say nothing to Mr. Muir. I should be very embarrassed to have to do so. Goodnight.'

She sat in front of her cosy fire that night, hands linked round her knees, and fumed. She'd like very much to march in to Mrs. Fenton's office and tell her she was resigning to-morrow morning. That would be for sheer personal satisfaction. But the fact of the matter was she couldn't bear to leave Fenton's at this stage ... though she wouldn't admit why, even to herself.

She told herself now that her salary made all the difference between just making ends meet, and living really comfortably. *That* was her reason for wanting to stay. Of

75

course it was.

But it was going to be hellish if she couldn't be natural with Nicholas Muir. She had an idea that Sarah would be watching them like a hawk from now on. That gossipy costing-clerk had a lot to answer for.

Virginia wondered why Sarah's quiet rebuke had hurt a lot more than Martha Warrington's furious tirade. Of course she had sensed something very personal in Sarah's attitude ... there was a very real jealousy there. Martha had been only protecting her son from potential fortune-hunters. I do have luck with the men in my life, thought Virginia despairingly.

Little things came back to her. Alison Marshall saying: 'I believe the boy-friend was up at Sarah's last night.'

The reply of the invoice clerk: 'Who? Oh, you mean Mr. Muir? Well, I daresay he has to keep on her right side.'

It was all very distasteful. Virginia got sick of her own thoughts and got a coat and, unlatching the french window, stepped out into the garden. The fountain was quite beautiful in the kindlier dark that hid the rust. Its tinkling water-music was sweeter than ever. There was a hint of early frost in the air and a shimmer of silver on the leaves.

She crossed the road to the riverside and walked briskly as far as Swann's Road Bridge, over it, back along the other side, and across Stanmore Road Bridge. By the time she got home her headache was gone and she could see the funny side of it, probably would make good copy some day, when the sting had gone out of it. Of course in a fictional setting, Leicester would immediately have appeared and allayed all suspicions, making for a much happier working atmosphere.

As it was, Virginia would have to see to any disarming herself. It was not fair to Nicholas otherwise. If he was at all involved with Sarah (she had to admit he might be) this could have made things awkward for him. Perhaps she should simply tell Mrs. Fenton how it had come about. But the trouble was, it was not simple. It was involved and artificial-sounding.

Besides, it meant dragging in Les Warrington again – and her own feelings regarding Leicester. Talk about it being wrong to 'kiss and tell!' It made her sound like a glamour-girl. It would do nothing to make Mrs. Fenton regard her as less of a danger. Gosh, and people used to think me slightly tame, thought Virginia, suddenly nostalgic for those days.

No, she wouldn't explain it, but how about letting Mrs. Fenton think she was practically engaged? No harm in that, surely? Virginia's over-inventive brain got busy. When her plan was perfected she went to bed and slept like a top. She turned up at Fenton's at nine-thirty instead of eleven-thirty.

Mrs Fenton said a brisk 'Come in,' to Virginia's knock, but she flushed a little as Virginia entered.

'I'd like a personal word with you, if I may, Mrs. Fenton,' said Virginia confidently.

Mrs. Fenton rose immediately and hung a 'Do not disturb' notice on her door.

Virginia plunged. 'I thought it was very kind of you to approach me as you did last night. I came to the conclusion that I ought to explain how it was that Mr. Muir took me out to lunch the other week.' She didn't give Mrs. Fenton time to protest that she hadn't known about that, and went on hurriedly, 'You see he thought he was rescuing me from an embarrassing situation.' She laughed. 'In actual fact he landed me in more embarrassment still. I'd like to explain fully, but it means dragging in someone else. Not fair to him. But in short, Mr. Muir thought he was someone else – he thought I was making excuses not to go out with someone I disliked. Nothing could have been further from the truth. He acted so impulsively that he made things very strained between me and – and—' Virginia contrived to look self-conscious – 'and someone – I well, rather like. Mr. Muir acted so quickly he positively whisked me away from what he thought were unwelcome attentions – or before I got my wits back. I think he felt really embarrassed over it when he realized what he'd done. And there the matter ended. He hasn't asked me out since, naturally. And I'd rather he didn't know you know about it. He'd feel an even greater ass.'

Mrs. Fenton gave a smile of relief. She'd spent most of last night wondering what Nicholas would say, how he would take it, if Virginia gave in her notice, and despite her promise, told him why.

Virginia noticed the relief and was emboldened to embark on the next stage of her story. Later she was to wish she had left well alone, but at the time it seemed to her that it would lend weight to her tale, and as Nicholas Muir wasn't here, wouldn't matter. He wasn't coming back till tomorrow.

'There's a favour I should like to ask of you in connection with that. My – my friend is a Presbyterian minister, so he can never get up for weekends, only during the week. So we get very little time together. I – well, if it isn't too much of a nerve, I'd like to have the afternoon off today to be with him. I thought if I came in two hours early I could get off early. It would make up to Leicester for the muddle-up last time.'

She coloured brightly, a convincing effect, that in reality was simply because she was not used to lying. Mrs. Fenton patted Virginia's hand kindly. 'Yes, yes, of course, my dear, I quite understand. A great pity Mr. Muir interfered. You go off sharp at one and have a full afternoon with him.' She smiled. 'But don't decide to marry him too quickly, will you? We very much value our advertising clerk.'

'No, I won't,' murmured Virginia, feeling a heel. 'Thank you very much, Mrs. Fenton,' and fled.

At one o'clock Virginia thankfully quit the premises. She walked into the Square for a bus and stood there quite undecided and restless. She just didn't feel like a session at her desk at the flat.

It was a glorious day. She lifted her eyes to the hills at

78

the end of the straight length of Colombo Street, and was lost. She hadn't climbed a hill since leaving Dunedin, where it was unavoidable. She saw a hills bus approaching and boarded it.

She knew the Cashmere Hills guarding the city of the plains were hills for hikers above the residential slopes at the foot, but she wasn't prepared for such an immense expanse of tawny-tussocked hillsides patched here and there with the blue-green of pines.

Right at the terminus was what they called here a resthouse – the Sign of the Takahe. When it had first been built, the *takahes,* a species of flightless rails, large, handsome birds with brilliant plumage, had been supposed to be extinct, but in 1948 a colony of them had been discovered in the unexplored-till-then forests of Fiordland. They were being carefully fostered and steps taken to protect them from the predatory, introduced animals that had almost obliterated them from the earth.

It was a building unusual for New Zealand, entirely Gothic in design, of stone quarried from the hills themselves and roofed with good Welsh slates. It had been raised by a man whose finest memorial it was, for the benefit of the hikers of the hills he loved so much, and with its heraldry, its coats of arms, its perfect attention to period detail, it seemed incredible that this man should never have seen at first hand the wonders of a period he wished to recreate in New Zealand for generations yet unborn. All this Virginia knew from a book Gwyneth had given her. Gwyneth often came up there, sketching.

Virginia went inside and did full justice to an excellent luncheon and lost herself in imagining she was dining in an English castle.

It was a tough three miles up to the next rest-house – the Sign of the Kiwi – and it wasn't long before Virginia discarded her jacket. At every bend in the road she paused for breath and to take in the view – sixty miles and more across a patchwork of plains, silver-threaded by rivers, to the long spine of the Southern Alps, reaching from north to south as far as the eye could see, and beyond.

Below the mighty watershed of the hills, bush-sheltered farms lay greenly in fertile valleys that widened into the plains.

At last she came to the crest of the road where it dipped down to the paua-shell iridescent waters of Lyttelton Harbour. There was a wide car-park for a lookout, and above the road lay the Sign of the Kiwi where people at little tables on the front terrace were having refreshments brought out to them. Virginia crossed the road to an outcrop of rock, and sat there in the sun, resting. When she cooled off a little she decided to go up the hill and get something long and cool.

As she crossed the road, she heard a car purring up from the harbour road and quickened her steps to get out of the way. Behind her she heard the car stop, a door slam.

She looked up. The sun was in her eyes. She had an idea this man might be going to ask her some direction. Not that she would know the answer. She put up a hand to shield her eyes, to bring him into focus . . . it did. Only too clearly . . . Nicholas Muir!

'My certes!' said the daughter of the Manse!

Nicholas Muir stared. 'So it *is* you!' he said. 'What in thunder are you doing away from the office?' As well he might.

If Virginia had looked hot before, she looked even hotter now. What in the name of ill luck had brought him here? And at this moment?

She gazed at the plains, at the mountains, back and down the Question Mark Road above Governor's Bay. She was seeking inspiration. Then she brought her eyes back to the manager's dark, brooding, even menacing gaze.

'Oh, what's the use?' she said bitterly. 'The craziest of things just happen to me these days! I just head out of one adventure into another. And I'm not looking for them, honestly!'

She was stalling for time, time to think, time to make something up. If she told Nicholas exactly what had happened, it would make things most uncomfortable, and besides, she had promised Sarah she wouldn't. She had a feeling he would be furious and march straight to Mrs. Fenton. Virginia bit her lip.

Nicholas saw that she was really distressed and took her arm.

'Get into the car, Virginia,' he said gently.

She knew an instant alarm. 'Nicholas, I'm not going back to the office today. I can't!'

He smiled, quite a nice smile. Virginia thought miserably, he might not be so nice to me soon – he'll think I'm quite, quite mad. And I am. Why couldn't I have left well alone? Just assured Mrs. Fenton I wasn't interested in Mr. Muir or him in me and left it at that. But no, I had to embroider the thing!

'I'm not going back to the office myself today. I'm not due back till tomorrow. We'll get away from this crowd and then talk.'

He headed the car towards Kennedy's bush. Given other circumstances Virginia might have enjoyed it, high above the plains and sea.

He pulled up by some old ruins, once another resting-house, the Sign of the Bellbird, and took hold of her hand.

'Now, what's the trouble? I won't eat you, I promise. Just be frank with me. Did you decide you couldn't bear to be indoors today? You've probably got a streak of the artistic temperament in you – I'll understand. Did you play the wag?'

Ah, that was an idea! Virgnia's fertile imagination caught hold of that. It would save them all embarrassment. She looked up, lips parted ready to speak, right into Nicholas Muir's brown eyes.

Then, 'No,' she said flatly, 'it wasn't that.' It was no use. For all his sophistication there was something fundamentally simple and honest about this man. She couldn't lie to him.

He looked and sounded puzzled. 'I'm not an ogre. I wish you'd tell me.'

'It's so – so damnably stupid and humiliating.'

He kept on quietly, 'I've done some incredibly stupid things in my time – and when I was younger, positively writhed over some humiliations. I asked you to be frank.'

Virginia said worriedly, 'I promised Mrs. Fenton I'd say nothing to you.'

'Mrs. Fenton?' His eyes narrowed. Then he said, 'Virginia, some people have a passion for making or demanding oaths and promises. I'm convinced they've made an awful lot of trouble in the world. People hate breaking promises, naturally. But sometimes it's a choice of two evils. And in this case it's either you tell me, or I'll go straight down now and ask Sarah what the deuce is up.'

Virginia gazed at him in horror and unknowingly clutched his lapels. 'Oh, you mustn't. Then she'd know I was alone.'

He stared. 'Know you were alone? What on earth – look, Virginia, you either tell me pronto, or I ask Sarah.'

Virginia gulped. 'Then I'll have to tell you – because it would humiliate her more than it would me. And make a stupid situation even more stupid and confused.'

'Well?'

She kept her head down. 'I—well, it was just that Mrs. Fenton heard about us . . . going to lunch together. She told me that you have trouble with some of the girls – being single – and that she doesn't like staff and management mixing.'

She paused as Nicholas said something under his breath. She didn't – quite – catch what it was, and perhaps it was just as well.

'Go on,' he said grimly.

'At first I was mad clean through – I felt like walking out – after all, I could make do on my free-lancing, only—' She cut that off. She'd nearly said she didn't want to leave Fenton's and he might ask why. She wasn't quite sure herself – yet. 'Well, I was so cross I—'

'You cleared out and have been walking it off ever since?'

'No,' a reluctance sounded in her voice. She wished it had been just that, but Mrs. Fenton might easily mention

82

to Nicholas tomorrow that she'd given Virginia the afternoon off to meet her near-fiancé. Oh, what a mess! 'No, Mr. Muir. It was last night at closing-time she told me this. I did try to walk it off – round the river – last night. I kept thinking how awkward for you it would be if Mrs. Fenton thought you were – well, interested in me . . .'

She felt his hand tighten. It was oddly comforting. Virginia was looking straight ahead at the Southern Alps, not at him.

'I found myself wishing Leicester might appear on the scene, to allay her suspicions. I'd have flaunted him under her nose. Then I had an inspiration, or so I thought. I wish now I hadn't. I thought I'd pretend the man I was all but engaged to was coming to town today and that would throw her off the scent. Then I asked for the afternoon off to be with him, you see. She was as pleased as could be. I went in early and worked this morning. And I didn't feel like going back to the flat and working – oh, if only I had! – so I came up here. That's all.'

She stared miserably ahead. Nicholas said nothing. This was horrible. Perhaps he cared for Sarah, thought he'd have to soothe her – in that case was he likely to feel hurt or exasperated with Virginia, or what?

He burst out into a great guffaw of laughter above her head. Virginia looked up, amazed, then she too saw the ridiculous side of it and was overcome. Finally, they sobered up.

'Virginia Jane Fergusson, you'll be the death of me! It's that imagination of yours. You've a positive genius for getting into ridiculous predicaments. How can you think of such things, even? Worst of it is, I seem to be going the same way. First of all you rescue me from the job I hate most – advertising – then I proceed to rescue you – *from the wrong young man*. Now, because of that, Mrs. Fenton seems to think we're in imminent danger of having an affair! Well, where do we go from here?'

'Straight home – each of us – but separately, I should
83

think. If you drive me home, after this coincidence, I should think every car that passed us contained Mrs. Fenton!' She paused. 'Unless you've changed your mind and are going to the office after all?'

Nicholas said, 'I'm certainly not. I'll have to wait till I've cooled off before I meet Sarah again.'

Virginia was surprised. He looked as elegantly nonchalant as ever. She said, 'How come you were coming back to Christchurch this way?'

'I finished up the business down south much quicker than I'd expected. I cut off the main road past Rakaia and came through Motukarara and Gebbie's Pass. I've got a beach-house at a little bay just beyond Governor's Bay and I've been building a stone wall there. I'm a bit of an amateur at it and I wanted to see if the mortar was holding the stones. It's not like brickwork. The stones are all uneven. I'm using them out of the hillside, lichen and all. That's an idea! We've both got to fill in the afternoon. Come on and see my beach-house. It's a glorious day for it.'

Virginia hesitated. 'What if Mrs. Fenton got to hear?'

For the first time Nicholas darkled. 'It has nothing to do with her. If she does – and I can't see how – I'll handle it.'

They swept down towards Gebbie's Pass on a road that was rough and winding and steep, where landslides in heavy rain were not unknown. These hills were greener because they faced the south, not the sunny north, and they swept down to the blue-green waters of the head of the harbour, remote and lonely.

Then they were running through valley farmlands where cattle grazed in the lush grass, and so came to a little bay. Now the houses were closer together and they had one mutual feature, netted orchards. 'Cherries,' said Nicholas. 'I must bring you here in spring when the blossom is out. Do you know that thing of Housman's?

"Loveliest of trees, the cherry now
    Is hung with bloom along the bough . . ."

Virginia knew a moment of deep enchantment. She loved people who quoted poetry naturally, as if it were part of their lives.

'Don't you know any more of it? Why did you stop?'

His mouth creased at the corners. 'Because it doesn't match New Zealand – at least the Southern Hemisphere. It goes:

"And stands about the westland ride
    Wearing white for Easter-tide."

And of course at Easter here the cherry-tree wears russet and gold – your colourings, Virginia. Your parents named you well, your colouring is just like Virginia creeper. I'm going to grow it over my wall.'

Virginia began to relax. She wondered what the beach-house would be like. She thought she could predict, knowing Nicholas and his with-the-minute knowledge of fashions. It would be flat-roofed and wide-windowed, with polished hardwood floors and Mexican rugs, gay and casual. There would be striped seersucker bed-covers and cream and orange cane furniture and long spotted glasses, bright awnings and deck-chairs.

Nicholas swung the car in over some cattle-stops and down a rutted farm track towards the sea. Ah, no doubt he had bought a section from a farmer; there'd be a concrete drive any moment.

They passed a bend where blue-gums and macrocarpas hid the bay, then suddenly they were in an old overgrown garden that all but overwhelmed the stone pioneer cottage cut into the hillside.

'This is it,' said Nicholas Muir, with evident pride. Virginia blinked ... not a sun-blind, not a landscape window. Not one modern note, in fact. A stone chimney, wreathed with ivy, ran up one side. The garden, a wild tangle, was a mass of honeysuckle, rambler roses, fuchsias and lilacs. Nasturtiums and sweet williams and candytuft had seeded everywhere during a long vacancy, she guessed, and the lawns had run into the flower-beds, save for a patch that had been recently scythed. It would take a colossal amount of work to get it in order, but what fun.

'I've only had it four months – came across it one day when I was tramping and was looking for a short cut to the bay. We'll have to go round the back. I left the front key inside.'

He took out a key that looked more like a castle key, it was so large, and fitted it into the old-fashioned lock.

There were not many rooms. There was a lean-to kitchen with an old black range in it, and a storeroom leading off it and a sitting-room that had a charm all its own. The fireplace almost filled one end, there was just room each side for a tiny round window, almost like a porthole.

The main window looked out over the harbour and it opened on to a narrow verandah. There were two bedrooms. The larger one had a cot in it as well as two beds. and there was a play-pen and toys in a cardboard carton.

'My sister Beth comes down here quite often,' said Nicholas. 'She has a four-year-old daughter Judith, and Peter is just eighteen months. You can't take children to hotels. Beth says this will solve their holiday problem for the next few years.'

It sounded so domesticated.

The other bedroom was obviously Nicholas's. Virginia's eye approved the books on his bedside table.

Back in the sitting-room, Nicholas went to a tall cabinet and produced glasses. 'I bet you're ready for a drink after climbing from the *Takahe* to the *Kiwi* ... to say nothing of getting all hot and bothered when I dawned on your horizon!'

Virginia hesitated. Nicholas took that for assent. 'I've got it standing in the well. I have got a fridge, but I turned the main off when I left. Always do. So there's no ice.'

He returned with two bottles of stone ginger! It was all Virginia could do not to laugh. It was deliciously cold.

He unlocked the door and took her out on the rather ugly old verandah. But the view!

'This was built almost a hundred years ago when Canterbury Province was only twenty years young. He was a

86

retired sea-captain and loved this view of the harbour, right from the shallows at this end, to the Heads.'

At the far end the verandah had been pulled down and here was the stone wall. He was going to build one each end, extending the width, putting down flag-stones for flooring and glassing it in.

There were to be built-in bookcases and a place for a desk and a comfortable chair at one end, he explained, and the other would hold folding chairs and tables where guests – if they became a necessary evil – could sunbathe, and where the kids could play. Virginia could imagine it as delightful in all weathers, and said so.

She could see the wall was Nicholas's pride and joy. He had built every bit of it himself. She glanced down at his beautifully manicured hands and at the rough-hewn rocks.

'I don't see how you manage to keep your hands like that when you work with mortar and rubble.'

'It certainly is rough,' he said. 'I had to have a special softening lotion made up to use on my hands.'

He glimpsed her expression as she turned away and he swung her back. 'You don't like the idea of a man fussing over his hands, do you?'

She said stiffly, 'I can't help it if I don't. I didn't *say* anything.'

'It's rather unkindly stupid of you, don't you think? You know I do the buying for the hosiery department? And you know what nylons are like to handle with rough fingers?'

Virginia nodded, shamefacedly, and felt the colour rise.

He looked at her with the brooding look. 'You know, Virginia, once or twice at the store, you've given me the impression that, although you work with them, you regard drapers as slightly effeminate. Isn't that intellectual snobbery?'

He was grasping her wrists so tightly he hurt them. His voice was stern, but looking up she perceived a smile at the back of his eyes. 'Perhaps I'd better demonstrate my masculinity,' he added, and kissed her, his mouth hard and

87

unyielding against hers. He released her, folded his arms, looked down on her and said, 'Well? What do you say now?'

Her colour was higher still, but she was game. She grinned at him and said, 'You win. You're certainly not effeminate.' She looked down the slope, anxious for a diversion. 'Is that a house-boat down there?'

'Yes, come and see my boat.'

The *Sarah Jane* was a trim craft with good lines. Virginia dared not raise even the fraction of an eyebrow over that name. Mr. Muir had an uncanny knack of reading one's thoughts.

'Sarah Jane was my mother's name,' he said suddenly, making Virginia mentally jump. 'She was like you, a bit of a lass, even if she belonged to a different generation. She led Dad a dance – never a dull moment. They were the happiest couple I've ever known, though it was fairly late in life that they married. So we lost them rather earlier than some folk lose their parents. Jane's your second name, isn't it?'

Their eyes caught and held. Virginia felt suddenly dizzy. How stupid! That was a very ordinary remark. Whatever could be the matter with her? And he was looking at her sort of oddly.

He said hurriedly, though why she couldn't tell, 'Would you like a run out in the launch?'

'Would I?' said Virginia, her eyes starry immediately.

'You'd better get into something of Beth's. I've got some old togs in the boat-house. You'll find slacks and sweaters in her wardrobe. She always leaves some here. No, she won't mind.'

The only pair of slacks Virginia could find were a pair of corduroys in a plum colour that contrasted vilely with her copper hair, but a cream sweater, high-necked, toned it down a bit. From the way Nicholas had talked of her, Virginia could have imagined Beth as short and plump, but she was evidently Virginia's height and much slimmer. Virginia had to hold her breath in to zipp up the trews, and she was acutely conscious of the way the sweater clung to her curves. However, it earned an approving glance from Nicholas as she ran down the track to him.

Out on the harbour there was a salt-tanged breeze and they could talk without embarrassment. Nicholas handled his craft well. Virginia stood beside him at the wheel.

He reverted quite naturally to their original topic. 'Sarah's a fine woman – she's had more tragedy in her life than most. She lost a little son of a year in tragic circumstances and three months later she gave birth to a daughter who lived just a few hours. She married a perfect rotter of a chap who finally took himself off – possibly a blessing. Though I feel Sarah still hankers after him.

'She's never divorced him. Then she was left some money, bought the business, and has made it her whole life these fifteen years or more. She's been gallant and gay, treats her staff well – and is most pitifully lonely. But—'

Virginia put a hand on his sleeve. 'Nicholas, you don't have to tell me all this.'

He took his pipe from his mouth and laid it down. 'But I'm going to explain, Virginia. I've partnered her to a good many things. I knew I was laying myself open to a good deal of conjecture ... a much younger man playing escort to a wealthy woman and all that, but I didn't really see why it should stop me helping her in that way. There's nobody in my life – as yet – to object to it. And she and I understand each other – or did. But now she's coming it a bit thick, it seems.'

He paused, then said, rather harshly and defensively, 'Of course in a situation like that, and amongst a big staff, all sorts of wild rumours get round. We've even been credited with living together – and who wants to believe that may!'

'I don't believe it,' cut in Virginia calmly and convincingly. She didn't know why. She only knew she knew it.

'Thanks,' said Nicholas, making no further protests, so she knew he believed her. 'That's Quail Island there. In my mother's day that was a leper colony. Then they moved out to Makogai in the Pacific. And now, of course, even in the islands there's very little of it. Wonderful, isn't it?'

Virginia shivered as they passed under the dark cliffs. She wondered what tragedies and fears and lonelinesses this small island had known. She was glad when they came out into sunlit waters again.

There were little coves to cruise round, and residential bays and silver-winged sea-birds dipping and soaring above them, and a coastal cargo boat was easing out of Lyttelton Harbour, a wake of foam-crested green water behind her.

Nicholas reverted to the topic of Sarah. 'She's not in the least in love with me, of course. I think she'll never love anyone but Terence Fenton. It's just that it's convenient and quite pleasant to have someone partner her to things – like the Master Drapers' Dinner the other week, and the Retailers' Ball. So I'm afraid she must have got to the stage where she would frown on anyone she thinks I might – might be interested in.'

'The solution's easy,' suggested Virginia. 'We have no need to see each other out of business hours.'

'I wouldn't allow anyone to become as possessive as that,' said Nicholas Muir. 'It would be inviting trouble.' Then he laughed boyishly. 'Just imagine, I might really fall in love with someone – what a complication!

'Besides,' he continued, giving her a teasing glance, 'I really would appreciate a change from Sarah. She *is* a bit old, you know. Oh, I'll still escort her where she wants to go, but she'll have to understand I'm a free agent. Besides, you're giving me a taste for adventure, Virginia,' he shot a laughing glance at her, 'and I really do think if we put on a show, it might stir up the laggard Leicester!'

He watched closely to see if she would resent that. She didn't – she merely poked out the tip of her tongue at him and said, 'You've already done that – you ought to have seen the letter I got from him yesterday.'

'Still, you don't want to fall into his arms right away . . . keep him guessing, girl. Besides, I deserve some reward for my assistance in the matter, and I'd no intention of letting the matter drop there. I was looking forward to – er – a spot of pleasant dalliance with you.'

He wondered how she would take that too. Damn silly thing to say, it had a touch of the Merry Monarch about it and—

'If it comes to that,' she said coolly, 'I wouldn't mind myself. I've never flirted before – and I find it quite extraordinarily pleasant. It's so nice not to have to be serious. I'm beginning to think real love is a bit of a bore. More pain than joy. It's not as if either you or I would take it seriously.'

'Of course not,' he agreed smoothly.

'I wouldn't dare flirt with anyone young – or – or inexperienced in—' she stopped abruptly.

'Or inexperienced in the ways of women,' he finished for her solemnly.

'I think it's high time we went back. I'll commit all manner of *faux pas* if we don't,' said Virginia. Then she thought of something. 'But if we do – go out together, I mean – Sarah will know – I mean she may suspect I was just telling her a pack of lies about having a near-fiancé.'

Nicholas said, 'Oh, you can safely leave Sarah to me. We'll wait a week or two. By then I shall have loosened the strings in such a manner she won't connect it with you. Then it won't matter.'

He was very confident. Virginia herself didn't feel half so easy.

When they had climbed the hill again, he took some supplies out of the car. 'I was stocking up for my breakfast tomorrow, but I've plenty really at my flat. Good job I did.'

Virginia cooked bacon and eggs on the ancient range while Nicholas toasted bread. She had another surprise when they sat down to tea. He bowed his head and said a quite old-fashioned grace. It was all she could do to keep from laughing – at herself.

'What is it?' asked Nicholas, sensing something.

Virginia wondered what he would say if she answered

91

'Oh, just that I'd tabbed you – originally – as a bit of a wolf, and your beach-house turned out to be so homely and you served ginger ale, not cocktails, and now you're saying grace.'

Before she could think of something to offer as an excuse, he said reprovingly, 'I know what you're thinking – that that's a quaint grace because I tacked on . . . "and make us more deserving." I know it's usually left off these days, but I like it – so does Beth – so Judith says it too. With so much hunger in the world it just reminds us. And might I add that for a minister's daughter you take the biscuit . . . laughing at a chap's grace!'

Virginia said hastily, 'It wasn't that at all, I was just wondering what on earth Mrs. Fenton would say – or think – if she could see us!'

They both laughed and he said: 'Well, I agree with you that the whole situation will be handled with delicacy and tact. I don't want her taking a set on you.'

After they washed the dishes they sat out on the verandah till the sun set and the twilight folded the hills in purple shadows.

'The lights will soon begin to twinkle on in the over-harbour bays,' said Nicholas, rising and stretching himself. 'so I think we should be on our way. I don't want you talked about.'

They raked out the ashes of the fire and left everything tidy. As Nicholas carefully turned that enormous key in the lock Virginia had a pang of regret. It had been so idyllic. Besides, tomorrow was looming up, and although Nicholas seemed to think there was no cause for alarm, Virginia was not half so sure.

CHAPTER FIVE

VIRGINIA left Nicholas looking appreciatively round her living-room while she went in search of Gwyneth. She found her in the studio in a paint-daubed and faded blue overall.

'No, I don't want to leave this at the moment, Virginia. Bring him up here, I like the sound of him.'

'You're honoured,' Virginia told Nicholas downstairs, 'she doesn't as a rule care for people to go up to the studio when she's working.'

To Gwyneth's relief he didn't comment on the picture she was engaged on. 'I've an interior study of yours in my flat,' he told her. 'I've had it ten years – first picture I ever bought. Got it at a Wellington Exhibition. It's called "The Leaping Flame" – a firelit study, yet with nothing in it save an old chair and a mirror and polished panelling, and you look at it a long time before you realize that even the firelight that dominates the whole picture is merely reflected firelight. So are other things you've brought in, the reflection of a brass bowl and a table set with crystal.'

Gwyneth smiled. 'That's the bowl on that shelf there.' She nodded towards it. Nicholas was delighted to meet it in the original. 'I've lived with it so long,' he said. No wonder Gwyneth liked him!

Gwyneth said, 'Perhaps you'd like to bring me up some coffee when you make it, Virginia. I'll have it black and strong with lots of sugar tonight.' Gwyneth was extremely varied in the matter of coffee, her preferences differed with her moods. 'And if you just happened to be making sandwiches, I might say I'm ravenous.'

Nicholas put a match to the fire Virginia had left set while she cut cucumber sandwiches. 'I always dream after them but can't resist 'em.'

Nicholas picked up the book of verse he had given her

from where it lay face down, but open, on a table.

'How've you got on with this?'

She was quite frank. 'Some of it I might understand in ten years' time when I'm more experienced, and some of it I just loved. Here's one, for instance. "Parting." It's haunted me ever since I read it. And the next one, "The Bond," I've read over and over, savouring every word.'

Nicholas read them both aloud. They were silent for a while, then Virginia picked up the coffee-pot. She simply must make a move. She didn't want to. This hour had been pure peace. And she knew there wouldn't be another like it for some time, because Nicholas wanted to straighten things out with Sarah before they went out again – if they ever could be straightened out. If Sarah was possessive and if Nicholas was wrong about her. Women had fallen for younger men before now.

'I'm just going to see if Gwyneth would like another cup,' she said as she started for the stairs. He opened the door for her, and stood there, waiting for her to come down again.

When she was at the top of the stairs, the telephone in Gwyneth's hall rang. She looked down. 'Would you answer that, Nicholas, please? It's bound to be for Gwyneth.'

It wasn't.

'Hullo,' said Nicholas.

'Hullo,' came Sarah's voice along the line to him! 'May I speak to Miss Fergusson, please?' Then, sharply, 'Who is *that* speaking? Is that you, Nicholas?'

'It is,' said he nonchalantly.

'Oh,' said Sarah in an ominous tone.

Nicholas swallowed and tried frantically to think what to do. Then he managed a casual tone. 'Did you want Miss Fergusson? I'll call her. She's upstairs in the studio with Mrs. Morgan, the artist friend she lives with.'

He immediately wished that unsaid. It sounded Bohemian. He couldn't very well start explaining that Gwyneth was a friend of Virginia's parents and a grandmother.

94

'I certainly do want her,' said Sarah tartly. 'The ad for the morning paper is all wrong, and they're holding things up. They got in touch with me. The one they've got is for Tuesday's paper and it's no good at all for Friday trade. It's full of country tweeds and brogues; the Friday one is evening wear and accessories. I certainly don't think Miss Fergusson had her mind on her work today. How on earth could she mix them up?'

'She may be able to explain it, Sarah,' said Nicholas easily. 'I'll call her.'

The 'Sarah' had confirmed Virginia's worst fears. She was standing frozen with horror at the stair-head. She set the coffee-pot down and descended slowly. As Nicholas met her at the foot she said unnecessarily, 'Sarah?'

He nodded and chuckled. 'The fat's properly in the fire now – but not to worry, we'll survive. And what have you done with Friday's ad? The *Banner* seems to have got next Wednesday's.'

Virginia said wrathfully, 'It's all that ginger-headed Murphy's fault. He said if the Wednesday one was ready he'd take it too. I didn't want him to do that. I like one clear before the next goes in. But he persuaded me, said they were having a re-shuffle and he wanted to work on them tonight.' She moved on, unhappily, to the instrument.

Nicholas caught her arm. 'If Sarah begins to say one word that isn't strictly business, hand the phone over to me.'

He stood by. Virginia picked the phone up as if it had been a deadly viper. She managed to sound quite ordinary. She explained what had happened. 'So I'll get Mr. Murphy on the phone, Mrs. Fenton, and he'll just have to dash down to the office with it. I can't imagine why he hasn't discovered the mistake before now – he was going to be working on them, he said. Something must have stopped him. I mean he would hardly be starting on them at this hour.' And she immediately wished she had not underlined how late it was.

Before she could say another word, Nicholas was tugging

at her sleeve. She said, 'Before you hang up, Mrs. Fenton, I think Mr. Muir wants a word with you.'

She went to sit on the bottom stair, her head in her hands. This was the finish of her career at Fenton's, of course. She only hoped it wouldn't mean the same for Nicholas. Though as a fashion expert and the guiding business hand, he was far too valuable to dismiss.

She couldn't help but admire the calm way he reported on his Dunedin trip. You wouldn't have known anything had happened out of the usual. She did wonder what Sarah had said when he said, 'Oh, that? I'll go into that tomorrow, Sarah. Bit lengthy for the phone.'

Fortunately, at that moment Sarah had to say, 'Oh, bother, that's my door-bell. Whoever can that be at this time of night? And my housekeeper is out. Very well, Nicholas, or shall I ring you back when I get rid of whoever it is?'

'Oh, I won't be here,' he said airily. 'I was just on the point of going, only I got terrifically interested in Mrs. Morgan's paintings. I've got one at home. But I must let you go. Goodnight, Sarah.'

He hung up and turned from the wall. 'Phew!' he said.

At that moment Gwyneth emerged from her studio and kicked the coffee-pot clean down the stairs. She gave a gasp and steadied herself by the banister.

The crash did Virginia's feelings good. For the first time she understood how enraged people could fire china at a wall.

Nicholas inspected the mess. 'We've had quite a night,' he said, and remarked to Gwyneth that they were in a sticky spot over some advertisements, but no doubt they'd find things came out right in the end. 'Virginia is just going to ring the chap who mixed them up. Right, snap to it Virginia.'

When she had finished with the apologetic Murphy they walked back into the sitting-room and regarded each other solemnly. 'And so ends my career at Fenton's,' predicted Virginia. 'Well, it was fine while it lasted. Though if I continue with the crop of rejections I've had this week, I'll soon be looking for another job. But that isn't what worries me.'

He looked puzzled. 'Then what does?'

'You. Your position. It's a splendid one for someone your age ... what are you? – Thirty-two? Thirty-three?'

'Thirty-two. You were bang on.'

'And it's all my fault,' she said miserably.

He came across to her and took her anxious face between his hands. They were cool against her hot cheeks. He smiled down into her eyes. 'Listen, Virginia, I'm going to take a strong line with Sarah. I will not have her trying to monopolize my private time or becoming possessive. If there's the slightest hint about sacking you, I'll threaten to leave myself. Without wanting to sound vain, she won't dismiss me, you know. And we'll carry on exactly as we intended to, except now that Sarah knows, we won't have to wait.' He smiled down into her eyes and said: 'I refuse to be done out of my pleasant dalliance. I'll see Sarah first thing in the morning when you aren't there, and even if she's a bit stiff for a day or two, take no notice, it will soon wear off.'

He picked up his hat and was gone on his goodnight.

It wasn't the cucumber sandwiches that kept Virginia awake.

Virginia turned up, apprehensively, at eleven the next morning because she just couldn't keep away any longer. She wanted to know the worst.

'Good morning,' said Nicholas blithely, appearing in her office. 'Miss Wentworth, take this sheaf of stuff over to the *Banner* office, will you?'

Left to themselves, he turned to Virginia. 'Sarah's not in yet. I don't feel like ringing her. I'd like her to lead off.'

A tap on the door from his secretary announced the arrival of an Australian traveller. He shut his door and Virginia picked up a box of skin gloves and tried to wax lyrical over them.

She was busy with the corset buyer and the commercial artist on the staff who did all the ticketing and the sketches for the ads, when Nicholas's voice came to her on the house telephone.

'Would you come into my office, please, Miss Fergusson?'

When she got in he was doodling on his blotter. It looked ominous. He was doodling skulls and crossbones. He looked up, then plunged. 'She's just rung me. I'm to go out to her place.' He hesitated. Virginia said, 'Go on ... there's something else she said?'

'Not actually said. But – I thought she sounded weepy.'

Virginia was aghast. 'Oh, Nicholas, what have I done? She's such a lonely figure. I'd hate to hurt her. For all her money she's so pathetic. And this means—' she cut that off

Nicholas's eyes were watchful. 'It means what?'

Virginia looked unhappy. 'That – that she – that her feelings really must be involved.'

Nicholas looked as uncomfortable as any man might at that idea. 'God forbid,' he muttered. 'And I'd hate to hurt her – but I shan't be able to avoid it. Now look, Virginia, you're not to worry. You've only precipitated matters. If she was going to get possessive something like this was bound to happen anyway.' He grinned. 'I feel as if I'm going to my execution!'

At the door he turned and came back to her and pinched her woebegone chin. 'Not to worry, as I told you before. I was bored to death when you arrived in Christchurch. I'd decided to quit at the end of this year and go back to London. So what matter? If we finish up with a flaming row, who cares? I'll just go a bit earlier.'

Virginia was annoyed with herself because try as she would, her foolish mind kept dwelling on what would Christchurch be like without Nicholas Muir? How ridiculous, when she had only come here to make Leicester Gordon more sure he wanted her!

Lunch-time came and went. Virginia wouldn't leave the office. She pretended she had urgent work to do and just nibbled at a sandwich she sent a junior out for.

98

At two o'clock, Alison Marshall came in, looking important. 'Mr. Muir's just rung me to say he wants me out at Mrs. Fenton's with the order books and the Australian samples.'

'Oh,' said Virginia blankly, 'did he send any message for me?'

'Not a word.' Alison's tone held a note of triumph. 'He just said: "Bring up the stuff I've given you a list of, and take a taxi, sparing no time, there's a good girl."'

Virginia bit her lip and returned to her desk. By the time four-thirty came and there was still no word, she was sure Nicholas had lost his temper, given in his notice to Sarah, and was just tying up the tag ends of this order for Australia, so the travellers could go on to the North Island as arranged, that night.

Well, she wouldn't leave till he got back or she heard somehow. The shop was open till nine Friday nights.

At six he arrived, frowning. But his brow cleared as he saw Virginia still at her desk. 'Ah, I'm glad you stayed. I dropped Alison at her place and told her she could pack it in now. Everything's all right, Virginia. Sorry I couldn't ring you, but there was no privacy at that end, and I wouldn't risk it at this, with a switchboard. Look, I rang those two travellers and told them I'd get this order to them at six-fifteen at their hotel. Can you stay on till nine?'

She nodded. He went on, 'Well, I'll be back by seven. Order tea and sandwiches for us from the cafeteria, will you, and I'll tell you the whole thing then. I dare not stay now, as I've held these men up long enough. But I wanted to reassure you.'

Virginia had the tea-tray ready when he came back and had concocted a long task for Miss Wentworth, out in the shop. She had an expectant expression on her face.

Nicholas grabbed an engaged notice and hung it on the outside of the door and clicked the bolt over on the other one. He seated himself at his desk and sighed deeply but relievedly.

Then he leaned forward over it. 'Sarah has completely

forgotten us,' he said. 'Her husband has returned home!'

Virginia fell back as far as a straight-backed office chair would allow her and her eyes filled with sympathetic tears and relief.

'Oh, Nicholas! Was he nice to her?'

'Absolutely. It seems he's been in Perth the last few years. Ran into a padre there who changed his life. He made up his mind that he wouldn't return till he made good, so that Sarah might never think he'd returned because of her money. It was Terence at her door last night!

'And Sarah, poor Sarah, is in transports of delight. This she said to me, is Terence as he ought to be. He's taking her off for a second honeymoon tomorrow. He's got a big business he can't leave for long, and they're flying to Perth. I'll keep things going here, of course, till they get things sorted out. She never even mentioned last night – it simply didn't matter any more. But there were a hell of a lot of ends that had to be tied up. I sent for the accountant – he arrived at the double with stuff to be signed – phew, what a day!'

'Thank goodness,' said Virginia. 'I'm sure you won't feel like any more, but there's some stuff that should go in the mail tonight.'

He grinned. 'I feel like a giant refreshed. Lead me to it! It will be sheer pleasure.'

They worked at speed and harmoniously till all was done. Then Nicholas went out to see to the last-minute checking of the shop. Time enough to tell the staff Sarah would be in Australia for some time, on Monday.

Virginia waited while he saw the last of the staff out, then he took her out to his car. 'It's only nine-thirty,' he said. 'Last night was too hectic for words. I'll take you somewhere now where we can be leisurely – and dally.' He looked at her sideways, but saw no reaction. Trusting, wasn't she? Apparently the rumours at the store had not disturbed her.

'It's the Hills again,' he explained as they turned along the road to St. Martin's. He parked the car at the foot of the hills. 'We walk from here.'

Virginia looked ruefully at her heels. 'I can see I'll be

wise to keep a pair of flatties at the shop. You're so un-expected, Nicholas.'

But at first the road was tar-sealed, then it lengthened into a rutty track. She lifted her face to the heights above them.

'That's for daylight,' said Nicholas. 'That way lies Witch Hill and the Giant's Causeway. Tonight I'm taking you up here.'

They scrambled up a bank and paused at a barbed wire fence. She was lifted off her feet and put over it, in a flash. It surprised her. She hadn't realized he was so strong.

There was a knoll of pines and blue-gums ahead of them. 'This was a favourite haunt of mine as a youngster,' he said, 'we lived in St. Martin's.'

Virginia turned to him as they walked on. 'Were you rather a lonely little boy, Nicholas? At least I don't mean that exactly, but shy?'

'Yes, I was. But how did you guess?'

'Because you're so self-possessed now. So polished, so confident.'

He burst out laughing. 'That's too subtle for any mere male. I was like Kipling's cat ... walked by my lone and waved my long tail where I pleased. Is that it? Near enough, anyway. I was more interested in creepy-crawly things than in organized sport.'

'Creepy-crawlies?' Virginia started to laugh. 'Oh, you're so surprising. You surprise me on an average of once a day.'

The sheep track they were following led right into the darkness of the pines. Virginia drew nearer Nicholas. They went right through and stopped in the lee of the huge rock that sheltered them from the strong east wind off the sea.

'Thank you for bringing me here,' Virginia said softly. She leaned against the rock to get her breath. Nicholas caught her other hand and turned her to face him.

'Thus far we've had mostly excursions and alarms; don't you think we ought to start this pleasant dalliance?'

He tipped her chin up and began to kiss her slowly.

When they drew apart again, Virginia was breathless and

wanted to hide that fact. He wanted to keep it light, she was sure. What on earth was the matter with her? She had never felt like this before!

She'd always thought of love as meeting someone you knew you cared for and wanted to spend the rest of your life with. And that you'd *know*, beyond shadow of doubting. But Les, Leicester, and Nicholas all had – apparently – the power to stir her. She felt alarmed. Did she really know herself? Then she chuckled inwardly. Perhaps Mother was right. She wanted Virginia to have a bit of a fling before she settled down as mistress of a manse. My certes – and it wasn't as if it were spring. . . .

CHAPTER SIX

On MONDAY Les Warrington walked into the office. 'Good heavens, where did you spring from?' demanded Virginia, looking up.

'That's not a hospitable greeting,' complained Les, grinning.

'I mean – how did you know I was here?'

'Asked your mother. I've been out to your place two or three times since you left.' He grinned. 'Your mother's a good scout. She advised me to leave you alone for several weeks. Thought you would find your feet and know your own mind better if left severely to yourself. I don't suppose she'd approve of my telling you, just the same – daresay she wouldn't think it was in the same line of technique.'

Virginia was amazed at this evidence of family collaboration and deceit and said so. Then something struck her. She said, uneasily, 'You don't mean Mother – er – actually—'

Another grin. 'I'll help you out. You seem to be getting stuck. You mean, does she actually favour my suit? Yep! Well, at least she didn't throw cold water on it. I wonder if you know how lucky you are having parents like that. Both said it was over to you, and advised me that even if you turned me down again I wasn't to do anything rash.'

'Rash?' said Virginia, a little chilled.

Les burst out laughing. 'Oh, I don't mean blow my brains out. They don't do that these days. Messy business, anyway, and puts a frightful burden of remorse on the poor girl. But I thought I'd have another shot at you, and if you remain unmoved by my pleas, I'm going to England.'

Virginia giggled. 'You really are quite mad . . . charming, but mad. I suppose you were going to England on business in any case.'

'It's not business, it's speed-boat trials. And I'm going for an indefinite time. Unless, of course, you accept me, and we make it a honeymoon trip. In which case, I shall cut the trials to a minimum and trot round the cathedrals and castles with you. And if that doesn't prove how much I love you, what would?'

Virginia said severely, 'I suppose you realize that this is all taking place in working hours? After all, Fenton's don't pay me to sit here listening to proposals of marriage.'

'Well, what time do you finish?'

'I'm allowed to leave at four-thirty if my work is up to date – I was engaged on that basis, you see. I work only part-time – that leaves me free for free-lance stuff. But tonight I'm staying on till the shop closes.'

'Why?'

'I'm going out to dinner with someone who doesn't finish till five-thirty either – and then to a film – so I'm not going home.'

'Oh, pity. I'd hoped to take you out myself. Well, what about lunch tomorrow?'

Virginia nodded. She might as well. They could discuss nothing satisfactorily here and she must convince Les he was wasting his time. At least she knew the state of her heart concerning *him*.

Les was reluctant to go, since he was at a loose end. He stopped proposing to ask about business. Virginia told him, when he asked after Mrs. Fenton, that she was off on a second honeymoon and that the manager was in charge.

'Decent chap? How do you get on with him?'

'Oh, so-so,' said Virginia. 'Could be worse.' She wasn't going to give anything away to Les, especially as she hadn't mentioned this pleasant dalliance idea to her mother. She added: 'And I'd really be grateful, Les, if I could get on. You know how Warrington's always frowned on the girls chatting with friends.' At which propitious moment the door into her office opened and Nicholas Muir appeared.

He looked inquiringly at Les. Virginia wished him at the bottom of the sea. She said, 'Oh, Mr. Warrington is just going, Mr. Muir. He was my former employer in Dunedin.'

Nicholas put out a hand. 'Seeing you're not in Christchurch, we can regard you more as a colleague than a rival, I think. Would you care to have a look over the building while you're here?'

Virginia could have shot him, but she wouldn't even give him a reproachful look. She didn't want Les to know she and the manager met on any other than a business footing. And she wasn't at all sure what dare-devil Les might say.

She needn't have worried. It was Nicholas who said the wrong thing. He grinned and said, 'I've reason to be very grateful to you. But for you Virginia would never have left Dunedin, I suppose.' At Virginia's outraged look, he added, 'You see, we bumped into each other – she wasn't looking for another job – but I persuaded her to work part-time, and she told me the whole amusing story in lieu of a reference. By the way, though I very much doubt that she'll need a reference when she leaves advertising, I do think she ought to have one. Care to see to it?'

Les, smiling, said, 'We didn't send one to her manse address on purpose. We hoped that when she got over her wrath, she might come back to us. With her home in Dunedin she probably won't want to stay here always, and my mother is ready to eat out of her hand. She's talking of tempting you with a higher – much higher – salary.'

Virginia said coldly, 'I'm not in the market for open bidding, Les, even if it boosts my ego. I enjoy my work here more than I have anywhere, and I've my own flat and longer free hours. I miss my family, but honestly, it's hard to live one's own life in a manse. Now, if you'll excuse me, I'll get on with this typing.'

Nicholas said, 'Oh, there's nothing you can't cope with later – I would like you to accompany us, then have some afternoon tea with us in the cafeteria.'

Virginia swallowed. What on earth had got into him? But she didn't want to argue, because she definitely wanted Les to remain unaware that her relationship with Nicholas was anything but manager and employee. It would only egg him on if he suspected it.

Therefore she 'Yes, Mr. Muired,' and 'No, Mr. Muired' till Nicholas, to pay her out, said quietly, 'Oh, by the way, *Miss Fergusson,* I couldn't get seats for the particular film you wanted to see tonight, so I got them at the Regent, and we can go to the Avon on Wednesday night. Or would Saturday night suit you better?'

'I think Saturday night would,' said Virginia faintly.

Les laughed. 'So that's why she turned down my invitation for tonight?'

Nicholas said immediately, 'Would you care to come with us? I daresay you'd be at a loose end otherwise. How about making it a foursome? There's Mrs. Chester, one of the buyers – a widow, but a very merry one.'

Virginia found she was gritting her teeth, but could do nothing about it.

Nevertheless it was a delightful evening, finishing up in Nicholas's flat for supper. The flat was much more modern than his beach-house, yet very suitable for a bachelor and with a certain smart beauty too. Certainly no homely shabbiness here.

As Nicholas escorted Virginia home he said, 'Les got me to himself and asked if there was any chance of your having the day off tomorrow.'

'To which you replied, "No, our valuable Miss Fergusson cannot be spared," I hope?'

'I said that you could have it off. He wants to take you out on the Estuary in a speed-boat. He knows someone who has one at Pleasant Point. I knew you liked the water. I told him that if you like to come in at nine, he could call for you at eleven-thirty and have the rest of the day. It's a good forecast.'

Virgnia's amusement struggled with something else, something that was almost resentment. Very casual, wasn't he?

Yet after all, why should he mind her going off with Les? It certainly wasn't as if he himself was serious about her. She wondered about him. What manner of man was he, deep down? Just the butterfly type that Alison Marshall vowed he was? A fashion expert and socialite? There were men like that – who preferred the superficial pleasures, didn't want women taking them seriously. But he had been kind.

Nicholas said, 'Hey, don't go into a day-dream. What is it . . . lost in a trance at the thought of a day on the water?'

'No,' said Virginia simply, and untruthfully, 'just wondering what I could wear.'

Nicholas chuckled. 'True feminine reaction to any date! Oh well, it's what fills Fenton's coffers. As a matter of fact there's a box of sample sportswear we've just ordered from, in the buying-room. There's a very trim yachting suit in grey. Oh, no, it wouldn't suit you. Pity you've got red hair.'

Virginia said coldly, 'How odd . . . yesterday, when you took me for that run to Kaikoura, you told me you liked red hair.'

'Don't be so prickly. Of course I do. But this one was called "Sea-gull" because it's grey and black, with splashes of red – like the red legs of a gull. And red would be abominable with your hair. But, by jove, there's one that could have been made for you. Better have a look at it first thing. It's not too horribly expensive, and with your staff discount quite reasonable. It's called "Sea-opal," and is a lovely thing in blues and greens. It's just you.' He chuckled. 'Better take Gwyneth with you . . . she could paint you against the background of pines and masts and sky . . . wouldn't Warrington be pleased!'

She had to laugh.

She bought the suit next morning – a mad extravagance for one day, of course, and didn't admit even to herself that she bought it simply and solely in case Nicholas invited her over to Kohumaru Bay again.

Les gave her a wonderful day, speeding round the Estuary Waters where the Avon and Heathcote rivers meet. It was an Indian summer day, so bright it dazzled. The wings of the sea-birds were sword-bright as they soared against the cobalt sky and caught the sun, there were reddish cliffs beyond and tussock-gold hills, and black-green pines singing an eternal song with the surf on the far bar where the ocean met the rivers, whenever Les stopped the engine long enough for them to hear it.

Les said suddenly, 'I could have made this more exciting, but I promised Muir I wouldn't go above a certain speed, and that I'd see you kept your life-jacket on.'

Virginia was amazed, not so much at Nicholas laying down the law as at Les, wild Les, taking notice of him. There must be something about the man. Yes, it had been exciting enough, for Virginia, but it couldn't compare with that other day, cruising gently round the harbour, and nosing back to the quietness and peace of sheltered Kohumaru Bay. That was what it meant, Nicholas had told her. Sheltered from the fog.

She took Les back to her flat for tea. She smiled to herself over what Gwyneth would think . . . heavens, life used to be very tame. Virginia had known exactly where she was going . . . slipping gently into an engagement with someone who lived the same sort of life as she did herself. She hoped Gwyneth wouldn't think her a minx. Only there was safety in numbers . . . it gave you a chance to know your own heart. Or did it?

Despite everything, Les went back to Dunedin the next day as he had come. Virginia would not marry him.

'Then I'm to book a single cabin on the *Angelina Lauro*?' he had said.

Virginia had said, 'Les, it wouldn't be fair to encourage you. I'm quite, quite definite about that. Thanks for being rather sweet. You were a very good boss, too. But I can't feel that our ways lie together. You'll meet someone, some day, who'll be just right for you.'

Les had asked, with an unusual seriousness, 'Is it going to be Leicester Gordon or Nicholas?'

That had made Virginia laugh. 'Oh, Nicholas Muir isn't the marrying sort. Didn't you realize that?'

And despite her relief that Les had accepted her refusal, she went to bed slightly depressed.

Life settled down again. Virginia now reaped the reward of her first weeks of freedom when she had feverishly written hour after hour, in the strong hope that she could make her complete living at this game and not have to ask them for help at home. She bought herself a brand-new typewriter and no longer dreaded her ancient one breaking down in the middle of an important passage, and took out subscriptions to half a dozen new magazines.

Words came more flowingly to her these days and her dialogue was more crisp and animated. She didn't analyse this too closely. Though perhaps, she admitted to herself, it was because Leicester's letters were rather more ardent than they had been. He rang her long-distance quite often, too, and seemed not to reck the cost.

Virginia answered his letters, but not as promptly as she had once, and sometimes even answered two with one; she talked to him quite amicably and pleasantly on the phone, but Leicester knew there was something missing that had been there once. He thought of Nicholas uneasily at times; at others wondered if Virginia was falling in love with a career.

One thing Virginia had freed him from was his mother's dominance. She walked much more warily with him these days. He'd known, of course, that it was merely slightly overdone mother love. She wanted the best for him – or what she thought was best.

But at least she was not so sure of her own judgment and methods these days. It had given her a shock to read in the paper the night Virginia left Dunedin that she had had a novel accepted. It would have been much to her son's advantage – probably still could be, when Virginia simmered down – to have an authoress for a wife. Yes, an asset.

Nan, watching her mother, thought Virginia had been good for her. Trouble was, her mother didn't have enough outside interests, so concentrated on her children. She wanted Leicester to marry and settle down, but because her love had turned to possessiveness, she didn't want him to love any woman too madly. Nan corresponded regularly with Virginia, hoped they might still, some day, become sisters-in-law, and Virginia in turn saw to it that Nancy knew she was having a gay and amusing time in the cathedral city of the plains, because there was no doubt Nan would pass it on to Mrs. Gordon.

Virginia loved the work at Fenton's. They were a grand bunch of employees. That was due, in the main, to Nicholas Muir, who, although now an executive, never forgot he'd come up from the ranks. It was a case of, if the captain's happy, the ship's happy.

Only Alison Marshall remained unfriendly. Virginia knew why now. Her disparagement of Nicholas had its roots in the fact that she wanted him herself and had never made any headway. It was quite hard to be sorry for her. She fawned on him, tried to anticipate his every need. Virginia sometimes wondered why Nicholas put up with her. It was quite often evident that she tried him sadly.

One day he said to Virginia that Alison had an invalid mother to support. 'She's not had much colour in her life, so she tries to take the gilt off other people's gingerbread to compensate. She needs outside interests and is very introspective and a mischief-maker. She's a good costing clerk, though.'

The pleasant dalliance took the form of outings to the theatre, the cinema, long drives to all the places within reach of Christchurch that Virginia didn't know, and, to her amusement, long sessions at the museum studying bugs and butterflies.

He showed her some of the little secret non-touristy parts of Christchurch, paths deep with crunchy leaves and acorns under the great avenues of oaks and chestnuts that girdled the city, the lesser-known gullies, deep in the valleys of the Peninsula, where they would park the car and climb for a view ... the maples in the Millbrook Reserve turned into flame and the wishing-pool grew so choked with leaves that the one you wished on didn't float under the bridge to make your wish come true. He even took her with him to plant bluebells by the roadside under clumps of trees. 'It's been done in the city reserves and parks,' he explained, 'But ever since I went to England three years ago, I've done this – I like to see them growing wild.'

He even appeared before breakfast one Saturday morning and took her down to South Brighton, right down the Rocking-Horse Road and over the sandhills to see the sun rise out of the Pacific, but that morning he took Gwyneth too. Had prepared her for it the night before. And had said to Virginia, 'Much the best, I think, and Gwyneth approved. Very early to make a call. And I don't want anyone thinking it strange – thinking I was leaving, not arriving.'

Virginia said, 'Oh, I wouldn't have thought of that.'

Nicholas said: 'No, you've lived a sheltered life till now, infant, and in a manse at that. Now you live alone, you must be careful.' He'd paused and said, 'Why are you so surprised I'm a bit sticky about the conventions?'

'Just because you said once you didn't give a darn about what anyone at the shop said about you and Sarah.'

He looked down on her broodingly. 'That *didn't* matter. But I've no wish to see *your* good name sullied.'

It had been a magic morning. The three of them had stood entranced, watching the black silhouette of the ferry steamer making its way against the golden east into the haven of Lyttelton Harbour and revelled in the colour and light and the salt tang in the air.

Sometimes Nicholas took her to a service in Christchurch Cathedral. Often she slipped into Holy Trinity at Avonside, just along the river from Gwyneth's Grace S. Richmond house, making her way quietly and reverently up the shadow-dappled avenue of silver birch, and rather enjoying the solitude of worshipping alone and not having to think she must remember to ask after all the ills of various parishioners.

Yet at times nostalgia would sweep over her for the Scots psalms that had always been part of her, and she would go further, along Bealey Avenue, to Knox Church, and feel at one with her people in the home church in Dunedin, as she sang with the others. 'I joyed when to the house of God, go up they said to me ...' Yes, that was what worship should be, a joy....

Nicholas came into her office one Tuesday morning. 'Miss Ambrose isn't in this morning, and I've a representative from Auckland with a range of evening frocks. You're much about the same size. Mind if I run a tape round you?'

Virginia stood up. Nicholas measured her bust, her waist, her hips, all with a most impersonal air, and Virginia was rather annoyed to find herself so aware of him.

'You'll do,' he said. 'On your way to the buying-room collect Miss Farne and Miss Thompson from the showroom and they'll show you the box of slips and the rest of the doings. You may need a strapless bra with one or two. Let's see ... ah, you've got high heels on, good. They look ghastly with flatties.'

Virginia was enchanted with the suggestion ... any girl would be. Much nicer than just describing them. And she had a warm feeling at the thought that Nicholas would see her in creations that promised to be ravishing.

Miss Farne and Miss Thompson were experts at deftly garbing her in one after the other, hardly disarranging her hair one wisp, and Virginia thought it the most fascinating way of spending a working day. Until mid-afternoon, that is, when her back began to ache, and her feet, and all she wanted to do was flop.

But the last rack revived her. These were dreams. There was a sapphire and silver lurex that shimmered as you paced, an emerald taffeta whose very rustle was seductive, and a russet bridesmaid frock in embossed velvet that turned Virginia into the very spirit of autumn.

Nicholas said: 'We'll get the Goldsborough girl into the shop to look at that one. She's going to be married in winter, with nothing to be spared in the way of expense. She's wearing old ivory velvet herself ... this would be lovely for her one bridesmaid. There are three child attendants. Perhaps pale gold? Make a note, Miss Farne.'

A ruby-coloured moiré was a superb gown, but clashed vilely with Virginia's hair. She asked if she could take it off quickly, please, and to do justice to the frock, how about a brunette trying it on? Nicholas and the traveller laughed. Nicholas took down the last. 'You deserve this, it's much more you. The pick of the bunch, in fact.' He smiled at Virginia, 'Didn't you say to me once that you thought it was time we swung back to fuller skirts, that women walked more elegantly in them? Well, this has got a little hint of that – a very slight Tudor air. That stiffened hem does it – swirls out. Better, I think, for walking in and dancing in than those swathed styles with a bit of leg showing – like that emerald taffeta or the lurex.'

Virginia vanished through the fitting-room door. She reappeared and paused, a hand on each side of the door to steady her, because she was so tired and the two men were examining something, their backs to her.

They swung round together and looked at her. Never before had she seen such admiration in any man's eyes. Her tiredness left her as if by magic, and she advanced towards them.

The taffeta was topaz-coloured and the waist had a pointed inset and was heavily embroidered in self-coloured raised padding stitch to match that swirling hem. Into each flower centre was sewn an emerald green brilliant. Large gold clasps set with the brilliants were clasped at the corners of the wide square neck. Her green eyes sparkled above them.

Nicholas suddenly swooped on a pin lying on the floor, and carefully placed it behind his lapel. Miss Farne was in raptures.

'Mr. Muir, when we have the mannequin parade next month, we really should have Miss Fergusson in that gown.'

'We'll certainly include her in the parade,' said Nicholas, 'but I don't know if we'll have her in that. We've never had a redheaded bride yet. What would you say to that, Miss

Farne?'

Miss Farne turned to Miss Thompson. 'She suits that Tudor style perfectly. How about that Elizabethan bridal frock in stiffened brocade? The off-white one.

Nicholas said instantly, 'No, not the off-white,' and added quickly, 'It should be dead-white with Miss Fergusson's colouring. And lace – soft, not stiff.'

Virginia hardly heeded them. She felt shattered. Nicholas didn't like her in this. Yet Virginia had never loved anything so much as this topaz gown. And it was beyond question that Nicholas's taste was expert.

Nicholas said, sensing her inattention, 'You'll take part in the mannequin parade, won't you?'

She shook her head. 'Sorry to be disobliging, but I don't fancy it. I'll write the script and love it, but somehow I don't fancy taking part.'

Nicholas twinkled, 'Oh, well, perhaps you don't feel it's quite the part of a future minister's wife, is that it?'

Virginia went scarlet. The other two women looked interested but puzzled. It was common knowledge that the manager took Virginia out.

She said hastily, 'It was nothing of the kind. Besides—' she left that, wisely . . . you couldn't start denying things here. This was business. She said, in a flat tone, 'May I get out of this now, please?'

'Yes. And afternoon tea is coming on, so get into your own things. I'll get – let me see – Berenice Clayton to try that ruby moiré. But that can do afterwards.'

Virginia then returned to her own office and made up time.

Presently the phone rang. Nicholas's voice. 'Would you be able to stay till half-past five, and come out to tea with me?'

'No, I wouldn't. But thanks.'

He chuckled, maddeningly. 'It was base, I know, to give your secret away, but I couldn't resist it. It just came over me. Do come, Virginia. My sister Beth has just rung to say she and Jack would like to go out tonight and would I baby-sit. She said if I had intended taking you for a moonlight spin or something – yes, she knows all about you – to bring you too.'

'But I wasn't going out with you tonight.'

'You weren't. But you will now, won't you, girl? I'll read you poetry after we get the kids to bed.'

Virginia gave in.

CHAPTER SEVEN

BETH was delightful, dark like Nicholas, but without his brooding look. She seemed to be possessed with amazing vitality. Jack was in direct contrast, broad and fair, with an air of placidity and an endearing drawl.

Virginia, the moment she saw Beth, could imagine her serving French salads and light-as-feather soufflés. She was therefore amazed when Beth produced a solid-looking but delicious steak-and-kidney pudding and an apple pie with cloves and cream.

'Peter, thank goodness, is already in bed and asleep. Thus far I've contrived to keep Judy clean till your arrival, but I won't answer for her from now on!'

Judith was adorable. She wore such an angelic expression that it seemed impossible she had even a speaking acquaintance with dirt. She was four, had an aureole of golden curls with tiny pink bows nestling in them, and a blue spotted frock with shoulder frills that served to add to the angelic air. From the reception she gave him, she evidently adored her Uncle Nicky.

'There's a new sort of spider in the fowl-house,' she informed him.

'Is there really? We'll go right down and see it.'

'Goody, it's got a funny stomach.'

Her mother wailed. 'Nick! I'm just putting the dinner out. And whatever will Miss Fergusson think? I don't know why my daughter had to inherit your love of bugs and beasties! I wanted a little girl who played with dolls.'

Nicholas tweaked Beth's ear. 'You're really secretly proud of it. Judith will make her mark in the world of natural science some day. I was too busy earning my living in the rag trade. And Virginia is only Miss Fergusson in business hours.'

He took Virginia's elbow and Judith's hand. Virginia

protested, 'Nicholas, I'm not in the least interested in spiders.'

'You will be . . . you've got to be.'

Virginia jeered, 'Imagine *you* – the immaculate fashion expert, keen on insects! It's right out of character.'

'In fact, almost respectable,' he countered. Then to Beth, 'Virginia persists in regarding me as a cross between a lounge lizard and a wolf.'

Virginia pushed him out of the door and followed him.

'It's a kind we haven't seen before,' said Nicholas to Judith, peering up into a cobwebby corner. 'I wonder if that abnormal stomach is peculiar to its type or some obscure spider disease.'

'Perhaps it's expecting,' said Judith solemnly.

Nicholas looked startled for a moment only. 'Oh, they don't have 'em that way, Judy. They lay eggs. As you can see, Virginia, my sister believes in telling them young.'

It was eight-thirty before they could settle down to the poetry-reading. Judith had insisted on a pre-bed romp. Nicholas had vowed he heard Peter crying and had got him up too, a Peter who was as adorable as his sister, with sleep-rosiness on his cheeks and dreams in his eyes.

The romp was so boisterous Nicholas lost his debonair air. Virginia was so sure they'd be too excited to sleep, she told them a couple of bedtime stories in the firelight, till Judith nodded off against Nicholas's shoulder, and Peter yawned widely. They carried them upstairs and tucked them in.

Nicholas went to get the book of poetry out of the car, but came in with a large parcel too. He cut the string and out of a sheathing of tissue paper shook the topaz taffeta.

'This could have been designed for you, Virginia. Would you take it as a gift?'

'No, but thank you. One of the things Great-Grandmama Fergusson said on her death-bed was: "Little Virginia, never accept clothes from a man. It isn't done." '

'I thought you wouldn't. Don't blame you, but I thought I'd try it out. Well, if you like to buy it you can have it cost price.'

Virginia hesitated, but only for a moment. 'I can't resist that offer, but when I'll wear it I don't know. But it's a dream, a fairy-tale frock.'

'I've got ideas about that. You know it's a holiday next Monday? How about paying your parents a surprise visit? I'll put up at a hotel. The opera company that's been here is starting there. You know how it is with an overseas company. They ask the first-nighters for formal dress if possible. You could wear the taffeta then.'

Virginia's eyes were starry. 'Oh, I'd like that above all things. You are rather a dear, Nicholas.' She caught his hand and squeezed it. 'You think of the loveliest things.' She looked up into his face. 'But, Nicholas, this afternoon you gave me the impression you didn't like this frock.'

Nicholas smiled down on her. He had no intention of telling her she had almost bowled him out when she appeared in it, that he'd had to conceal his feelings from the others by picking up that pin, and that he had felt a great distaste at the idea of Virginia wearing that frock at the parade for who knew how many men to gape at. It sounded so unreasonably primitive, and he had always thought of himself as an excessively civilized sort of chap.

He said, 'Well, I wanted you to have it for next Saturday night.'

Virginia thought this demanded some return. 'Sorry I was churlish about being in the parade. I – I think I was just childishly disappointed that you didn't like the topaz one. So I'll do it, if you want me.'

'Just if you think Leicester wouldn't mind. '

Why did he have to bring Leicester into tonight?

She said soberly, 'It's nothing at all to do with him.' Then she added, 'But I loved the sound of that Elizabethan off-white brocade. But you didn't, did you? Why?'

Nicholas smiled into her eyes, that smile that made Virginia feel a little breathless. 'Well, it's a fair question, deserves a truthful answer. Because I fancy pure white for you. Because I think your parents named you well –

Virginia.'

She was glad she didn't blush because it was very nicely said. In that instance she knew he wasn't a wolf, that although he was enjoying this romantic interlude, he would keep it light, and expect no favours from her that she wasn't prepared to give.

It was a long trip to Dunedin, even though Nicholas left the accountant to see to business in the store at night, and he and Virginia left at six after a light tea at the cafeteria. They encountered a slip on the road past Palmerston and patches of fog on the motorway, so it was after midnight when they dipped down the last hill to the city.

As they swung into the Bay road Nicholas said, 'I'd better tell you now that I've already met your people, Virginia.'

She stiffened with surprise. 'You've – but how could you?'

'That last time I came down to Dunedin. I had dinner with them and spent the evening too.'

Virginia was amazed. 'Aren't parents deep? I'll have something to say about this! What with never telling me Les had been visiting them – and now this. Really!' Then she grinned. 'It's probably just as well. I forgive you – and them. Otherwise, if I arrived with a strange man in the wee sma's, they might wonder what had happened to me. I used to be so circumspect.'

Virginia rang the front door-bell and called out. As Mr. Fergusson appeared in dressing-gown and pyjamas, she flung her arms round him, realizing just how much she had missed them.

Then her mother came down the stairs, her chestnut hair glinting in the light and a warm blue dressing-gown clutched round her, her eyes shining like a girl's. No wonder Dad adored her still.

There were ecstatic greetings for a while, then they all trooped off to the kitchen, which would heat up quickest. Mr. Fergusson, with a sleepy idea of being helpful, seized a loaf and began cutting thick slices. His wife snatched it away from him. 'I believe he thinks it's the breakfast toast he's doing!'

'Well, why not toast?' asked Nicholas. 'We had a very light tea before six, and only an apple since.'

'Yes, I'm starving,' said Virginia. 'Fingers of toast with melted cheese for me.'

'You'll dream, my girl,' said her father.

'Well, I like dreaming,' said Virginia. 'Besides, what about those enormous bacon-and-egg suppers you and Mother used to tuck into after church on Sunday nights when you were first married?'

Her father smiled. 'You know far too much about us! All right.' It was good to have her home again.

The door opened and in came Richard. Virginia flew at him and he submitted to her hug with brotherly fortitude.

'I thought I heard sounds of wild revelry downstairs. Gosh, Virginia, aren't you the dizzy limit arriving at this hour and not letting us know you were coming! You've wakened me up!'

'Ah, but are you awake?' demanded Virginia. 'You look bleary to me. Why not just toddle off to bed again – you'll be asleep again in two twos. If you stay here eating you'll be worn out in the morning.'

She removed the plate of toast out of his reach. Richard stretched out a long arm and collared a piece.

Mrs. Fergusson came back with a pile of sheets and pillow-cases and proceeded to stack them on the hot-water cylinder.

Virginia blinked. 'I won't need all those.'

'There's just two pairs, one for your bed and one for Nicholas's.'

'Oh, Nicholas isn't staying here. He said he was going to ring the Southern Cross as soon as we got in. Nicholas, you ought to ring them now.'

Mrs. Fergusson looked shocked. 'He'll do nothing of the kind. Virginia, you sound most inhospitable. After Nicholas bringing you all the way down for a lovely surprise for us!'

She looked across at Nicholas where he sat at the other side of the table with her daughter. 'You'd like to stay here, wouldn't you?'

'I certainly would,' said Nicholas, and spared them any inane remarks about putting them out. He looked sideways at Virginia. 'Don't you want me?'

Virginia had the grace to blush. 'Of course I do,' she said, 'it was just—'

'Did you think it might upset Leicester . . . or Leicester's mama?'

'No, I did not. I thought we might not be – well, grand enough for you, that you might prefer a hotel – I did you an injustice, sorry.' And she touched his hand for a fleeting moment under the table in a gesture of apology. Nicholas's fingers instantly closed over hers and would not let them go.

She had to use her other hand to pick up her toast. Mother had a twinkle in her eye. Virginia was sure she knew. She suddenly realized an awful thing ... Mother was taking Nicholas seriously *and he was the one she favoured*.

This was going to be awkward. It would be very difficult to explain to one's mother that one was just indulging in a spot of pleasant dalliance and finding it gorgeous fun. Fun? Well, mostly. Sometimes one was conscious of an ache.

'Let's all get off to bed,' she said hurriedly, and seized the sheets. Mrs. Fergusson and Virginia made up the spare bed while Nicholas brought in the luggage and unpacked his.

'I'll show you where the bathroom is,' offered Virginia, picking up her own sheets. 'I share a room with Penny. You've met our Penny, I suppose? What particular role was she playing when you were here?'

Nicholas grinned. 'She was getting round in shorts and a khaki shirt and wishing she'd been born a boy.'

'Oh, well, that one lasted longer than most. You've no idea what we've been through with Penny. She's had these violent and cranky enthusiasms ever since she was about five. How the parish puts up with her, I don't know. She just emerges from one phase to go into another—' she pushed open the door '—and she looks so angelic when she's asleep we forgive her anything.'

The light from the door struck across Penny's bed and she sat up, rubbing her eyes. 'Is that you, Virginia . . . oh, how beaut! Gosh! Is that the Nice Man?'

'Are you?' Virginia asked Nicholas.

'I hope so,' he said, walking across to the child's bed.

'Penny Fergusson!' cried Virginia, 'what in the name of fortune do you think you're wearing?'

The last time she had seen her little sister she had been wearing boys' striped pyjamas. Now she was sitting up in bed with a wisp of primrose nylon and satin ribbon slipping off her skinny twelve-year-old shoulders.

'It's – it's – one of your nightgowns,' Penny said, in a tone of one making a discovery. 'But you see, Virginia darling, I hadn't got any nightgowns left. I'd grown out of the others meanwhile.'

'But what's wrong with your pyjamas?'

'Too masculine. What's the use of women being women if they aren't feminine? How else can they express their true personality, their right destiny?'

Nicholas changed a guffaw into a cough and nearly choked himself. Virginia sighed deeply and said, 'Well, if that's the case, okay, but if you wear gauze at this time of year you'll get your death of cold.' She opened a drawer and took out a fluffy bedjacket. 'Look, this is feminine enough for anyone . . . it's even got true lovers' knots on it.' She draped it round Penny's shoulders. '—And listen, chick, I don't mind you going all feminine, but not in my best nightie. You can return it to me tomorrow.'

'Well, will you make me some nightgowns? But not plain sensible ones. Mum says you can't get exotic ones for children.'

'Yes, I'll make you some, all frills, but there'll be more of them than that one of mine. Now cuddle down. It's after two.'

Nicholas bent down, laughing. 'Good night, Penny.' He kissed her. Then he went on just as casually to kiss Virginia. Virginia propelled him hastily to the door. 'You utter idiot!' she hissed. 'That'll be all over the Bay School – with embellishments – on Tuesday morning.'

'Didn't I pick a good place?' he drawled, and kissed her in the hall, right outside the bathroom door just as Mr. Fergusson came out of that door.

Virginia felt dismayed. Who likes to be kissed by a man in front of her father? Nicholas chuckled. 'I seem doomed to kiss you in public tonight. She made me come out here, sir, because of Penny.'

The two men went off together laughing, leaving Virginia glaring after them.

The week-end certainly had its awkward moments as well as its highlights.

Nicholas was drying the morning-tea dishes while Penny washed them. Virginia had been down with the list of hymns for the organist. She came through the kitchen where her mother was slicing beans and she could see the others' backs as they busied themselves at the scullery sink.

Penny's voice floated out to them in all its youthful and devastating assurance. 'I'm so glad Virginia has taken up with *you*. You're so different from Leicester.'

Virginia gazed at her mother in horror. Nicholas's reply was indistinct. Virginia did not know whether to fold her tent and silently steal away or to cut in with a sisterly 'Dry up!'

So she did neither. She just stood. Penny continued: 'Of course he's a good guy. An absolute wizard at sport as well as having bags of brains . . . I do like a man to *be* a man, don't you? But he's so young.'

Nicholas said, and to his credit there wasn't a trace of a laugh apparent, 'Well, at least no one could accuse *me* of that.'

'Oh, no,' Penny was quite unaware of irony. 'How old

are you?'

'How old would you think?'

'About forty, I'd say.'

Nicholas was wise enough to see the compliment implied, knowing full well all that the very young want is to be taken for older, and he confessed to a mere thirty-two.

'Never mind, you look older than that.'

'Thank you.' Nicholas rinsed the dishcloth and mopped up the bench, seeing Penny had gone into a day-dream.

'You're really quite domesticated, aren't you? What a husband you'll make.'

Virginia decided it was time she chipped in, 'Yes,' she said coolly, 'isn't it a pity he isn't the marrying kind?'

The pair at the sink swung round. Nicholas's eyes did not meet Virginia's. They met Mrs. Fergusson's and there was a smile at the back of each pair of eyes that made Virginia wonder.

She said hastily, 'Still, even a confirmed bachelor needs to have something of the domestic arts. Help is hard to get.'

Nicholas laughed. 'Oh, I have a part-timer. But I keep her by reason of being a tolerably tidy fellow. And my mother saw to it that Beth and I shared the chores equally.'

'I approve that,' said Mrs. Fergusson. 'When Richard and Virginia were small we were in the country and I managed to get some help, but when Penny came along there was no chance of it. I tried to keep on my parish work too, and the result was that when she was six months old I was ordered a month's complete rest. We didn't want to keep Virginia off school, so my husband took over, even to changing the baby and doing her washing.'

Virginia left the room smartly. Really, the family were hopeless. Fancy talking of such sordid details as changing babies in front of a man like Nicholas!

She suddenly giggled to herself. It was all part and parcel of Mother's make-up. Someone had once said of her that she had the knack of seeing the best side of everybody – complex things were quite simple to Mother. She didn't see Nicholas as the playboy type at all, sophisticated and experienced. She simply saw him as a lonely sort of lad who'd never had the good fortune to get married.

The phone in the hall rang as Virginia passed. It was Nan Gordon. 'Listen, Virginia. I was speaking to Mrs. Bertram this morning and she told me you were home – said she'd seen you over the fence. It just happens Leicester is here too for the long week-end. Some former minister is visiting his parish and agreed to preach there. He's on his way to see you. He's got seats for the opera. Do go with him, Virginia. I'll tell you a secret. He's got three seats and was taking Mother and me. As soon as Mother knew you were in town she offered to step down if you would go with him instead.

'I thought I'd tell you so you'd know you've got Mother eating out of your hand now. But for heaven's sake don't tell Leicester *I've* been shoving my oar in. He's had more than enough of interfering relations.

'He told Mother that if you wouldn't have him he was off to England. And I've got to thank you – this has given Mother such a scare that she's stopped interfering with Geoff and me at long last. And she's such an old duck when she doesn't.'

Nan stopped at last for want of breath. Virginia said, 'Nan, you are a darling. I'll drop round some time to have a few minutes alone with you. There's something I want to ask you. Oh, Leicester has just passed the window, I'd better go. But I'm afraid I'll have to turn him down – not out of spleen. It's simply that the manager of Fenton's brought me down specially to take me to the opera. He's taking the family too. Sorry – 'bye for now!'

Leicester was more than a little surprised when he walked in the back door to see Nicholas and Penny sitting on the table.

Mrs. Fergusson went on slicing the beans, struggling with laughter. Leicester looked up to see Virginia in the doorway.

'Hullo, dear,' he said possessively, and strode across the room and bent to kiss her as if it were his right. Virginia had only time to turn her cheek, so that it landed very lightly. Mrs. Fergusson really had trouble now, Penny looked furious and Nicholas only amused.

Virginia said: 'You've more or less met Nicholas, haven't you, Leicester?'

Leicester sounded suave. 'More or less just about described it. He whisked her from under my nose. I think he thought I was pestering her.'

'I thought you were Les Warrington, not Leicester Gordon,' said Nicholas, calmly. 'After all, I find it hard to keep up with all Virginia's suitors! Then, when Les really did arrive, I got all soft-hearted on it and let them have a day off together. But even the chance of honeymooning in England didn't move her ... so poor Les is going alone.'

Virginia decided she'd better get Leicester out of it. When Nicholas was in this mood you could do nothing with him. She walked into the hall and Leicester followed. He brought up the question of the opera.

'I'm sorry. Nicholas is taking Penny and me and the parents. Richard is off on a moonlight hike with some other medical students.' She paused. 'You could always take your mother.'

Leicester gave her a reproachful look. 'You're a brat!' He took her into his arms. 'Crowd in the kitchen cramped my style.'

The study door opened and Mr. Fergusson came out. 'Ahem!'

'This house!' said Virginia. 'Not an atom of privacy!'

'No,' said her father coolly and meanly, 'even last night you were finding it difficult, weren't you, my darling daughter!' He tweaked her ear. 'I saw you pass the study window, Leicester. How about taking the evening service for me tomorrow night? The folk always like to hear a minister who grew up in the congregation.'

They went into the study to discuss the order of service.

After tea they were sitting round the drawing-room fire,

all reading. Nicholas fitted well into the household. It was exhausting to have to entertain people the whole time, but Nicholas simply got a book and settled down.

Penny suddenly appeared as a vision in frilly white. Her glossy brown plaits were tied on top of her head with a demure blue bow. She was trailing a length of blue moiré ribbon.

'Would you tie my sash for me, Mummy, please?'

Virginia thought how sweet her little sister looked. She had an appealing oval face with pointed chin and wide cheekbones. She had darkly blue eyes, a sensitive mouth over pearly small teeth and really exquisite eyebrows – and was as tough as they came.

But sister-like, Virginia said nothing of what she was thinking. 'Last time we took Penny to the Repertory first night she had to be forcibly dissuaded from going in corduroy slacks and a sloppy joe. Are those my nylons you've got on?'

'Yes,' admitted Penny, lifting her arms for her mother to pass the sash round. 'I hadn't any left. I had to tuck the toes under, though. Pity you've got such big feet, Virginia.'

'I take exactly one size larger than you,' her sister retorted with heat. 'And another thing ... what do you mean, pinching my Enchanted Evening perfume and filling the bottle up with diluted vanilla? I refuse to go to the opera smelling like a fruit-cake!'

Her mother said quickly, 'I've a new bottle not opened. Your father gave it to me last birthday. And a very glamorous one.'

'No need,' said Nicholas. 'I've got some for her, but I hadn't got round to giving it to her yet.'

Virginia's eyes softened as she looked at Penny. 'You look rather bare about the neck. Would you like my triple pearls?'

'Would I? But won't you want them?'

Virginia turned a little pink. 'No, I've got a cameo on brown velvet.' Her eyes flickered to Nicholas. He smiled at her across his book. He had feared she would not have accepted the cameo had she known it was a family possession. So he had said nothing.

Presently Nicholas and Virginia went upstairs to change. Nicholas turned at the door to have another look at the fireside group. 'Looks quite Victorian and charming ... Penny on your father's knee in her white frock and blue sash and those black pumps.'

'Daddy's so thrilled to have a little daughter again after that excessively tomboyish stage, he gladly bought her that party frock.'

Half-way upstairs Nicholas paused and felt in his pocket and brought out a small phial. 'I know there are lots more exciting kinds, but I'm funny that way. I don't care for anything but lavender water on my women. I always buy Beth this.'

There was a little smile at the back of Virginia's eyes. 'You are a strange mixture, Nicholas – in some ways so sophisticated and man-of-the-worldish, and in others so conservative. I think I rather like it. It's sort of endearing.'

She raised herself up by his arms and kissed his chin. Then she ran up ahead of him to her room.

The family liked the topaz taffeta. Virginia saw her mother's eyebrows go up when she saw the cameo, though. Mr. Fergusson could not take his eyes off his daughter ... the square, low-cut neck, the heavy costume jewellery repeating the green of her eyes, the swaying skirt with its glittering hem. He sighed a little. Virginia was all a woman now.

They sat quite near Leicester's party. There was some magic abroad tonight. Virginia couldn't remember another night like it. ... Voices that carried one far into the realm of music, music that stirred one's pulses and set a throb in the heart ... the passion and power of the story, Nicholas's eyes meeting hers occasionally in appreciation of some tender passage, his fingers tightening over hers now and then.

'I hope you don't mind,' he whispered once. 'I'm holding Penny's hand, too.' Penny had slipped it into his at a tense

128

moment she only half understood.

They stopped for a few moments in the foyer to chat with the Gordons. Virginia would have been less than feminine had she not slightly exulted in Mrs. Gordon's definitely subdued air. She never dreamed I'd ever look at anyone else but Leicester. And she would have ruled us all our lives and spoiled our marriage. I'd have resented it and taken it out on Leicester. Virginia gave a very real shudder at the thought.

Back home Mrs. Fergusson had left coffee and sandwiches ready. She'd evidently prepared them beforehand. 'Penny, you can have yours in bed – then get out and do your teeth – and seeing Father has a service at ten tomorrow morning, I think we'll do the same, take ours up, otherwise we'll sit here till all hours talking it over.' She whisked the surprised minister away before he had time to protest.

All very pointed, thought Virginia with deep chagrin. It meant her mother regarded Nicholas as her new young man! She looked across to where he was lighting a cigarette. 'Nicholas, I'm awfully sorry. The whole family seems to be taking it for granted you're—' she faltered. 'I – I mean they—'

Nicholas helped her out, his lips twitching. 'You mean they're accepting me as a suitor for your hand. Well, what matter? Won't it just spur Leicester on?'

Virginia turned quickly away to hide the pain she was sure was revealed in her eyes. Nicholas went swiftly across to her, took hold of her. 'Darling girl, I'm not in the least embarrassed. Don't worry. What else could you expect your family to think? I can't very well say: "Look, I'm just dallying for the sheer fun and pleasure of it." Now can I?'

Virginia's brow cleared. He had not noticed her distress. She must take this as lightly as he. She laughed and the green lights danced in her eyes. Nicholas leaned over the couch and switched the standard lamp off. He turned and poked the fire into a blaze. He looked mischievous. 'It doesn't matter if I crush your frock now, does it? Have I told you just how beautiful you look? Excitingly beautiful?' He whirled her off her feet and sat down with her. His brown eyes were looking into hers quite seriously. What a good thing she knew he was only fooling!

'Virginia, I found a poem the other day that might have been written to you, you green-eyed witch . . . it began:

"I have loved green, the green of lovely things,
    The pale, flat discs of new nasturtium leaves . . ."

and finished up:

"But the green wonder of your laughing eyes,
    Stirs me, each time, O love, to new surprise." '

Leicester had sometimes read poetry to her, he had certainly never quoted it for her alone. Virginia wondered, not for the first time, why, oh, why it was that men who could be so delightfully polished and satisfying in lovemaking should seldom be the marrying sort?

Despite the hour Nicholas had gone to bed, he woke early, feeling a giant refreshed. The Fergusson family were decidedly stimulating to a palate that had been definitely jaded till a few weeks ago. It was going to be a sparkling day with a hint of frost.

He turned and surveyed the bookshelves beside the bed. Most of the books he had read. There was a thick black book on the bottom shelf. He opened it and there across the front page, in Virginia's untidy scrawl, was written: 'Virginia Jane Fergusson: Her book.'

Of course he should have put it down and asked permission to glance through it later, but he very badly wanted to see what sort of poetry the young Virginia had liked and written. It was simply crammed with quotations and poems and had been started in her last year at High School. It showed quite discriminating taste. It gradually developed into a diary of sorts, not written every day, but as the mood took her. He knew he ought to have put it down now, but the temptation was too strong. And some of it was so darned funny. There was the joyous start of a

University course, then the shadow of possible blindness for her father, the ray of hope that the operation in America promised, the hurdle of finance that had to be overcome. Nicholas could guess that Virginia had poured out all her frustration in this book rather than let her parents know how much it had cost her to enter commercial life and to turn her not inconsiderable talent to describing merchandise.

It was interesting to see how she had hated the shop at first, then mellowed, developed her philosophy. She had evidently had her ups and downs with the management, particularly Martha Warrington and a certain manager she had employed before Les was old enough to take more responsibility. Viriginia had worked off steam in rather vitriolic pen-sketches. Like this one:

'Mr. T. would have been Robespierre in another existence – the Sea-green Incorruptible! Even his suit has a greenish tinge. And he's cold, implacable, unfeeling. He sacked Joan today. He enjoyed sacking her. Pah! I hate cold people. If only he lost his temper I could forgive him, but he just sneers. Dad would say there was a reason ... perhaps he has a bossy wife. But is there any real need to spread unhappiness further?'

Nicholas turned a page. He didn't know what had occasioned this, and never would, because naturally he couldn't confess he'd read it. 'Drapers! A race of effeminate creatures in an effeminate trade! Give me men who really do something ... thinkers, students, scientists, ministers.'

Nicholas rather wryly returned the book to its shelf.

It was evening, and he was sitting beside Virginia in the Bay Church, listening to Leicester's attractive voice. There was much more to his preaching than just a charming voice, though. Nicholas soon recognized that.

His belief was powerful and compelling, with a modern approach to the old truths. He was speaking tonight on the theme: 'He that believeth shall not make haste.' At first he spoke of the things that do need urgency, that have an imperative need of action, the reforms we dilly-dally about, then urged a matching patience in the things that need slow, sure growth, that mature in the fullness of God's time. 'He that knoweth the end from the beginning. He that maketh the crooked ways straight.'

Nicholas wondered if everyone in the church was automatically reviewing their own life even as he was. As they rose to sing, so fittingly, 'Not so in haste, my heart . . .' he caught the look that came, momentarily, from pulpit to Virginia. He did not turn to look at her. That moment was Leicester's, he deserved it – something swift and intimate. Every word spoken during that sermon – even if Leicester himself had not meant it to – might have drawn them closer together. Perhaps Leicester was purposely not making haste . . . perhaps in his slower way he wanted Virginia to be sure of herself. Because marriage was for life. Or at least that was the ideal. Sometimes it couldn't be that way, and two people had to pick up the pieces and make a fresh start. But with these two it would be for ever.

Mrs. Gordon and Leicester were invited to the Manse for supper.

Mrs. Gordon declined, saying she could get a lift home with her neighbour. Virginia thought of the times she and Leicester simply could not get a moment to themselves and suppressed a smile. Penny was in bed, flat out to it, after an unaccustomed late night, and Mrs. Fergusson had the supper ready. After it, Leicester drew out cigarettes and offered them.

'I'll take mine with me,' said Nicholas, rising. 'I'm going for a walk on the beach if I may be excused. I'll just let myself in if you're all abed.'

He walked round the bay, glad of the strong nor'-easter that blew in across the harbour and brought a tang of salt to his lips. Around the curving beach he came to rocks jutting out, and when he climbed up them to see if there was a track to the next bay, he found there wasn't, but there was a hollowed-out part that gave shelter from the freshening wind, yet afforded a wide view of the deserted bay.

Well, one didn't really wonder at Virginia preferring professional men. She'd been brought up amongst them ... law students, medical, divinity. They had something, certainly; their speech was deep, their confidence something that sprang from their own specialized knowledge. Not that he'd ever felt a lack till now ... he'd thought his reading had filled in the gaps. It had been so necessary when his mother was widowed for him to find a well-paid job, that didn't need years of training. Oh well, life was very amusing, and weren't eavesdroppers supposed to suffer a certain fate? So it seemed did people who peeped into other folk's diaries! Best just to take what came one's way, and be philosophical about it ... in this case, pleasant dalliance. It would be something to remember.

Leicester asked Virginia to come to the gate with him. She said, 'Yes, I was just wanting some fresh air myself. I'll go after Nicholas.'

They stood at the gate, sheltered a little by the arch cut in the *matipo* hedge. Before Leicester could speak Virginia did. 'Leicester, I don't want you labouring under any delusions. Please don't make your mind up about me. I don't even think I'm the one for you. I'm going to be candid. I don't think you've ever got over ... Melanie.'

Leicester snorted, 'Would I have tried to make you marry me if I hadn't?'

'Yes, I think you could have. She's gone out of your life and I came into it. And plenty of people settle for second-best. But I won't.'

Leicester laughed. 'Virginia, are you a tiny bit jealous of someone I cared for ages ago? I'd like to think you were.'

Virginia's voice was sober. 'That's the trouble, I'm not. I'm being frightfully and coldly analytical about it. I knew

133

there was something missing in your feeling for me. I sensed it – the sort of thing that perhaps you're only capable of giving once.'

Leicester didn't answer right away. Then he said, 'Can two attractions ever be the same? Is there only one way of loving? This could be more real, more substantial, more lasting.'

Virginia said in a small voice, 'But not so satisfying.'

Leicester said, 'How can I convince you? Virginia, this is how real it is to me. If you don't have me, I can't stick it at Greenhaughs alone. I'll go to England at the end of the year. You've got till then.'

Virginia spoke quickly. 'That's not fair to you. I'll tell you now, then you'll be free, know where you are.'

Leicester refused that. 'I think you're still carried away by the freedom you're experiencing. I won't take no for an answer – yet.'

... She couldn't see Nicholas anywhere on the beach and was about to go back, thinking she'd missed him, when she saw a spark among the rocks and went swiftly along the hard sand left by the ebb tide. She peered up. 'Is that you, Nicholas?'

He sprang up, reached down a hand, and helped her up. They sat down, Nicholas with a protecting but casual arm around her. Virginia had a white scarf tied over her hair. She peered at the circle of cigarette butts. 'Did you really smoke all those?'

'I did.' Even his voice sounded withdrawn.

She peeped up into his face. 'Did you – tell me true – feel a bit out of it tonight?'

'Nobody made me feel out of it, Virginia, but I did feel that Leicester was more in the picture after a magnificent sermon like that.'

Virginia wasn't sure what he meant, and didn't know, either, that he was still smarting under that scornful: 'Drapers!' but she sensed a hurt somewhere. 'Oh, Nicky!' she said, and laid her cool cheek against his. It was the

134

first time she had ever used the diminutive of his name. Surprised at herself, for daring, she turned his face round, kissed him lightly on the lips – and the next moment was seized and kissed anything but lightly.

She wriggled round and put her hand in his coat pocket. He said, 'What on earth are you after? Lost your hanky?'

'No, just after your pipe. I'm sure it must be here – yes, it is. I don't like you chain-smoking. I'd rather you had a pipe in your mouth. It looks more contented, more like you. I'd like just a quiet, peaceful half-hour here with you.' She turned her face under his chin. It was as much as she could say. A girl couldn't make the running.

A week later she was sitting in her office gazing with loathing at a garment in front of her. It was a large affair of coutil, satin, webbing, heavily reinforced with spiral steels and front lacings.

'Why the savage look, Miss Fergusson?' asked Nicholas, dropping some papers on her desk.

'Just imagine having to wax lyrical over ghastly contraptions like these!' She lifted it by one sturdy suspender. Nicholas did not, as she expected, grin back. He looked stern.

'That's just the trouble, you *don't* wax lyrical!'

'What do you mean, Ni – Mr. Muir?'

'Your corsetry ads are the only ones I can find fault with. The buyer came to me the other day and said that though she felt every other department had had a lift since you took over, hers were very poorly worded.'

Virginia flushed. 'It's easy to get lyrical over ninons and satins and laces and bows . . . but these things!'

'I suppose you've never worn anything like them?'

'I should say not. What do you—'

'So just because you look as slim as a willow wand, you can't be interested in the things experts in their own lines have devised to make women of heavier build, with sagging muscles, able to feel well-groomed and foundationally right for smart ensembles!'

Nicholas's tone was really cutting. Virginia looked dismayed. Put like that it sounded mean. She opened her mouth. 'I – I—'

He cut in. 'I had an advance note yesterday advising me that one of the corset firms is going to conduct a week's night-school in Aubery Chambers, if we would like any of our staff to attend. I think you'd better go along with the salesgirls. We can't have one particular department suffering simply because you're snooty about their goods.'

Virginia blinked, but Nicholas had gone into his own office and shut the door. She smarted all day.

At night she was glad to shut out all thoughts of the shop and start an article. Oh, what freedom! Thought of some of the articles Virginia was expected to describe gave her a pain in her fifth rib! Free-lancing was sheer joy.

There was a tap at the french window – Nicholas. 'Want to go for a spin to the sea?'

'Too cold.'

'Yes, I'd noticed the atmosphere was decidedly chilly. It's not like you to sulk.'

'I never sulk!'

'Ah, that's better. Flashing eyes and hot cheeks suit you much better than icy disdain, Virginia!'

Virginia giggled. It wasn't possible to stay mad with him.

Down Wainoni Road they drove, over the Bower Bridge, and down to North Brighton. They walked north along the beach into solitary ways. Viriginia began to feel better, she loved the sea-wind in her face, the moonlight making a path, right to their feet, across the sable waters.

They walked, it seemed for miles, then found a sheltered sandhill to rest on before walking back. Nicholas lay back, his hands under his head, and considered the stars.

Virginia sat with her knees drawn up and gazed at the sea.

'Breeze blown away all the cobwebs, Virginia?'

'Yes, all gone. Oh, bother, I've got an inspiration and for once I've no notebook and ball-point. Have you?'

He had. Virginia scribbled away, filled one side of the page, and turned it over, writing fast.

'Poem?' asked Nicholas lazily.

'No. Just listen.'

He grunted and sat up. Virginia spread the paper out on her knee to catch the light of the moon. 'Corsetry. Ah, the very name smacks of tight laces and whalebone, doesn't it? And that's what it was till modern corsetières took it over. And now ... supple spiral steels, light as feathers, elastic webbing as filmy as gauze, and seamed satins control those hitherto uncontrollable muscles and add enchantment and curves where enchantment and curves were lacking.'

She paused. 'There, that's as far as I've got, Nicholas. What do you think of it?' then, suspiciously, 'What the devil are you laughing at?' For Nicholas had collapsed on the sandhill and far from praising this effort, was convulsed with mirth. 'What a girl!' he howled. 'I bring her out for a spot of dalliance and she prattles of stays! Stays, mark you, under a moon that Helen of Troy would have found irresistible!'

Virginia got to her feet and surveyed him wrathfully. 'You're most inconsistent! You just about reduced me to tears with your sarcasm today – and when I do get hold of something you laugh!'

She went to put her hands into her pockets and as she did the paper fluttered to the sand. She stooped quickly just as Nicholas bent for it. 'Thank you,' she said, holding out her hand.

He shook his head. 'No, you're in the mood to rip it up. I'll probably appreciate it tomorrow in the prosaic atmosphere of the retail world.'

'Oh, please give it to me. I wrote something else on that – on the back. I'd rather you didn't read that.'

'Oh, sounds intriguing. Let me see.'

Nicholas was holding the paper away from her tantalizingly.

She went cold. 'Nicky, Nicky dear, please! Do please understand. I hate anyone to read any of my unrevised poems. I like to have them word-perfect.'

'Sounds reasonable,' said Nicholas, handing it back, 'as long as you let me see it when you finish it.'

'I will,' she vowed, without an atom of truth. 'Thank you.' She tucked it thankfully into her pocket. Nicholas kissed her. He seemed rather intense. Virginia had to resist an urge to kiss back. He looked down on her and she thought his voice sounded shaken. 'A kiss – like that – justifies a moon like that.'

Driving back, Virginia issued a challenge. 'You promised once you'd take me back to your place on the harbour. You never have.'

'I'll take you over some time when Beth and Jack are there.'

'Not by ourselves?' She sounded disappointed.

Nicholas shook his head. 'Wouldn't be wise. A future minister's wife has to watch her step, you know.'

Virginia was more than ever glad that that revealing poem was safely in her pocket.

CHAPTER EIGHT

ALISON MARSHALL had now become quite cordial to Virginia. Somehow Virginia thought she liked her better when she was frankly antagonistic. At times she felt Alison merely cultivated her friendship for the sake of saying nasty things about Nicholas.

It was very difficult for Virginia not to fly to his defence, but she realized she mustn't let Alison draw her fire. And it was decidedly unpleasant, anyway, to be put into the position of discussing him in any way whatever.

In the guise of this pseudo-friendship she said once, 'You didn't really take much notice of my warning, did you, Miss Fergusson . . . I feel I still ought to repeat that he's never serious about any girl. Just—'

'But what does that matter? I'm not serious about *him*. I don't hear wedding-bells, for instance, every time a man takes me out. Safety in numbers. As a matter of fact I'm going out with those two ad-men tonight, Peter and Murphy, exploring some of the night haunts of the city.'

Alison let her mouth fall open. 'And does Mr. Muir know?'

'Not yet, but he will. Now please excuse me, I must take these blocks over to him.'

Nicholas looked up as she came in. He was alone. 'Will you come to that film tonight?'

'No, sorry, Nicholas, it will have to be tomorrow night. I'm going out with Murphy and Peter McGregor tonight.'

'And what for, may I ask?'

'Their editor suggested they do a new column, just for a few weeks, longer if they can make it meaty enough. They're all for it – they're sick of ads. It's to start off as: Christchurch . . . a conservative city, or is it? Some phases of night life in the garden city.

'They don't want anyone in these places to know they're newspaper men and reckoned they'd be less suspected if they had a partner. So they're taking me, since I'm in the same line.'

'I'm not in the least impressed,' said Nicholas. 'I don't think you should go. Heaven knows what unsavoury dive you might get into.'

'Oh, don't worry. I don't think things are raw enough here. Christchurch is no den of iniquity, bar a few drunks and burglaries – and our own pet incendiarists, of course.'

There had been some daring burglaries, followed by fires, and the papers were making a splash of it; the police were making grand efforts and many business firms were uneasy.

Nicholas still looked thundery. He was very good at it.

'Well, I'll get seats for tomorrow night.'

She laughed. 'Fine ... unless of course I'm too exhausted by my descent into the underworld. They're going another night to a gambling-school they've got wind of and an opium den, but no women are allowed there!'

Leicester rang that night while Murphy and Peter were waiting for Virginia to get ready. 'Sorry, Leicester, but I can't talk for long. I've got someone waiting. No, not Nicholas, two newshounds from the *Banner*. We're copy-hunting. Night-life stuff – what did you say? Oh, Nicholas? Yes, he knows, but he's no more pleased than you are.' A pause, then, 'Oh, don't be absurd ... it may not be the thing for a future minister's wife, but that hardly applies to me. I'm a fancy-free maiden, with a literary bent, off snooping for news. Don't worry, you won't hear of my body being found in a warehouse cellar, gnawed by rats, or making the headlines tomorrow morning. 'Bye, Leicester.'

It was not *tomorrow's* headlines Virginia made. The night proved very tame, due, though Virginia did not know, to Nicholas going round to the *Banner* and threatening all sorts of things to Peter and Murphy if they dragged Virginia into anything messy.

Nicholas and Virginia saw an excellent film the next night, then had supper at a restaurant. Virginia grinned across at him. 'For all the copy we got last night, I might just as well have gone out with you. The only bit of action we saw was a police raid for after-hours drinking at eleven o'clock. And very tame too.'

'Served you right,' said Nicholas. 'And there's to be no more of it. By the way, I must call in at the shop. I left my pipe there – upstairs in the little reserve office. I'd like one before bed.'

He unlocked the side door off an alley, and carefully locked it after them, 'Otherwise we'll have some poor policeman charging in thinking we've been broken into.' Nicholas switched on the lights over the side stairs. As they went into the mantle reserve he reached out a hand to the switches inside that door. A fruitless click rewarded him. 'Bother, I forgot that switch goes off with the ones at the front. Never mind, I think I can feel my way over. I know I left my pipe on the table beside the house telephone. Will you wait here?'

'No, thanks. I didn't know reserves looked so ghostly with only the street lamps shining in – positively eerie with those models shrouded in wrappers.'

She put her hand in his and moved warily through racks swathed in dust-covers, steel T-stands, wooden hat-stands. There was a crash as Nicholas knocked something over. He stooped to right it. 'One of those plaster busts, and only today I put the fear of death into the showroom juniors about the way they were getting the necks chipped. I'll have to have chromium caps made for them. They show badly with blouses.' Virginia collided with some of the T-stands. 'Never mind, you can't hurt them.'

'No, but I've got new nylons on.' They reached the office door.

'Have you got it?' asked Virginia from the doorway. 'Men! They regard their pipe like their best friend.'

Nicholas stowed it in his pocket and turned. The moon was shining through a skylight. It lit up a mirror exactly opposite the office. It was only for a moment, then the fitful moon went behind a cloud, but that moment was enough to show Nicholas something ... two dark figures crouching beside the strong-room door!

He took hold of Virginia's arm and spoke loudly. 'What about a kiss, darling?'

Virginia got a slight shock. 'Whatever are you shouting for?'

He laughed, and spoke just as loudly. 'Do you prefer whispers for lovemaking?'

'I do ... soft music and low lights and all that.'

'Well, I'll start whispering sweet nothings if you like,' said Nicholas, still in that loud tone, then dropped his mouth to her ear and said, 'Don't say a word ... to give the show away. There are burglars over by the strong-room. If we continue to fool we can get out and give the alarm; play up like mad.' He laughed and gave Virginia a smacking kiss.

She achieved a laugh too, and said, not whispering, 'Come on, darling, it's stuffy in here. I hate that mothball smell too. Take me home.'

The journey back through the crowded racks and models was a nightmare. They laughed and joked as they went. 'Damn that bust!' said Nicholas with feeling as it crashed over again.

At the stairhead it was Virginia who spoke loudly, 'I've always wanted to slide down the banisters during work hours – now I'm going to!'

Nicholas hopped on the other side and in half the time they were at the foot. He unlocked the side door and locked it again. 'Virginia, I'm going round to the back. I think they must have got in that way. You go to Smithers' – they're still open – and get them to ring the police.'

Virginia hesitated, but only for a moment. 'You – you won't do anything foolhardy?'

'No. Promise. We may have disturbed them and they

may make a quick getaway. On the other hand they may think we suspected nothing. Now off to Smithers' *and stay there*!'

Virginia sped on tiptoes. She gasped to an astounded milk-bar attendant, 'Ring the police and tell them burglars are at the strong-room at Fenton's – on the first floor, that the manager is in the side alley!'

Back down the alley she flew, terrified of what Nicholas might do. At the corner she collided with a flying figure. She clapped a hand over her scream as she realized it was Nicholas. He spun her round, gripped her arm, and raced her back to the main street. Fearful of pursuit, Virginia ran like the wind.

Nicholas wrenched open his car door, thrust her in and got in himself. They were heading up Colombo Street before he said, 'They're making up Royston's alley. I heard them getting out over the bake-house roof. We may head them off yet. It was rotten luck them taking that way.'

Virginia decided she'd never tell Nicholas she thought he was fleeing from the burglars. He swung his car into a street at right angles to Colombo Street, just missing a parked car, and at that moment a truck came hurtling out and turned east. Nicholas slowed a little. 'I don't want them to have an idea – I don't see how they could have, though. I mustn't lose them.'

The streets were still fairly busy, so if they kept to town, no suspicion would be roused. The truck driver turned south at East Belt, then doubled back up Moorhouse Avenue to the Waltham crossing. 'Hope they turn in soon,' muttered Nicholas, 'otherwise they may twig us. Once they do, we can phone the police.'

'It couldn't possibly be a bakery van, could it?' asked Virginia. 'I mean, they do work later hours.'

'Little ray of sunshine, aren't you? Well, even if we look mutts at journey's end, we've got to stick to them. The police will understand, I daresay they too have to follow lots of false trails. But as that number-plate is decidedly muddy and obscured, I'm almost sure it's them. But that mud is drying and falling off bit by bit, you might get the number soon in case we lose it. I admit it would be an anti-climax to get a sinister-looking house surrounded by coppers and then find a perfectly respectable baker crawling into bed beside a substantial and flannelette-gowned spouse.'

'Substantial spouses and flannelette nightgowns being the acme of respectability, anyway,' said Virginia, beginning to recover a little from her fright, and realizing what wonderful copy this would make. Behind them in the city fire-sirens began to wail.

'Is that sheer coincidence, or have we really disturbed the incendiarists?' asked Nicholas grimly. 'Is Fenton's going up? But it's our duty to try to collar these chaps. Where is he going now? Very suspicious. We've come right round the Heathcote River and are going to cross the hills end of Colombo Street. If an ordinary driver wanted to get to here, he'd have turned into Colombo Street from the alleyway.' Then he groaned. 'If he heads up Hackthorne Road and takes to the hills, he'll twig us.'

But the truck continued past and went round the foot of the hills beyond the Princess Margaret Hospital. Nicholas said, 'I'm going to stop at the next telephone box and phone the police. There's no turn-off for a bit – and it will allay suspicion if we appear to have reached our destination . . . here's one . . .' He braked, said with a groan as the truck disappeared, 'And there's the last of the mud fallen and it's too far away. Never mind.'

He was in and out of the booth in a jiffy. 'Just said we could be making for the Main South Road, Hoon Hay Valley, Tai Tapu, Motukarara or Akaroa. Poor beggars, what a list!'

A quarter of an hour later they caught up again. Virginia copied the number down in case they lost it later. The truck was going much more slowly now. They were grateful to every car that came up and passed them, then they'd never suspect any one car. Nicholas looked at the petrol gauge. 'Oh, fine. Just as well I filled up tonight.'

They passed the turn off to Gebbie's Valley, and several other valleys Virginia couldn't put a name to, and now Nicholas was fairly sure it would be Birdling's Flat, or the township of Little River, or Akaroa itself. Further than that they could not go. The road ended in cliffs.

The miles slipped by. Nicholas said, 'Virginia, I'm going to try something out. There hasn't been another car for a time and they may get suspicious. I'm going to speed up and pass them. That's an old truck and they can't make time on these hills. Then I'll turn up one of these valley roads and hope they take me for a farmer going home. Then when we see them pass, we'll emerge and follow again. They'll think it's a different car.'

'I'm lost in wonder, love and praise,' said Virginia. 'You've got Murphy and Peter licked to a frazzle. Just wait till I tell them! I wonder if their editor would let me write this up.'

'And now, girl, you get over into the back seat and crouch down. Pull that rug over you.'

'Whatever for?'

'They'll be far less likely to connect me with that courting couple in the reserve if they see only one person.'

Not for anything would Nicholas have told her that in the glimpse he had had of the two men silhouetted against the moonlit sky as they crept over the bake-house roof, he had seen the light strike on something that was dark blue, steel, and evil.

There was little armed burglary in New Zealand, but if these fellows were the incendiarists, they were armed. They had wounded a policeman who had nearly caught them, and as, in the case of a house burglary in Papanui, an elderly man had learly lost his life and was still on the seriously ill list, they wouldn't want to be caught to face serious charges.

Nicholas accelerated, impudently sounded his horn, and swept past them. He maintained his speed, and a mile further on turned left into a valley road, in view of them.

Virginia said, a few moments later, 'Do you have to go

up as far as this?'

'I'll have to. They may know this part, and if they see our lights stop short of a farmhouse, they might wonder. We'll turn into the first drive we see.' There was one round the next bend. Nicholas was thankful it was long and winding. The house-owners would never hear them. He drew in under bordering pines and switched off. 'We'll watch for their lights between the trees. Come on out.'

Virginia's teeth were chattering, and Nicholas put an arm round her. 'You're cold.'

'No, only excited – and scared. Shouldn't they be past by now? You don't—' the next moment they froze. The truck was coming up this valley, not going past.

'Nicky, suppose they come here? What about the car? If this is their place. Can we get it out in time?'

Nicholas seized her arm. 'Doesn't matter about the car. We dare not risk them catching *us*. Come on!' He hurtled her across the drive. 'Quick, over to the fence.'

Virginia felt her frock rip as she got over. She couldn't have had a tighter one on. She pulled it free and tugged at Nicholas's hand. The fitful moon was no use to them. It only deepened the shadows where all sorts of pitfalls lay, Californian thistles, rocks that rolled, clumps of gorse and *manuka*. The trees and scrub continued right to the top of the hill.

'If they do turn up this drive,' he gasped, 'they'll stop as soon as they see the car and we'll have to stop crashing through this as soon as they do and lie low. I don't want them to know where we've gone. They might think we're prowling round the house.'

They reached the top of the hill and turned to look down, their hearts in their throats, their lungs tortured with their gasping breathing.

The truck came straight up that drive, passed it and continued up the hill. They let out great sobbing breaths of relief. On the still air they heard the driver change to low gear for the next rise, saw the lights disappear as they dipped into a hollow, then reappear, slow, and turn into the next driveway.

They watched the lights between the trees of that drive, heard a gate open and shut, a door bang, then a house-door, then, blessedly, silence.

They sat down and recovered their breath. 'And so the little burglars went to bed,' said Virginia, on a half-laugh.

'Now we must plan what we can do,' said Nicholas. 'I think we'd better creep down this blasted hill full of lawyer vine and clingweed and thistles and whatnot and push the car silently down that drive and round the bend, then drive like fury to Motukarara, or the first township or store we see.'

'You don't think we ought to find out if the homestead the car is in has a phone?'

'No, I can't risk it. The homestead might be a mile back, and if they're neighbours of this crowd they may pooh-pooh the idea. Or you never know, they might even be in with them. Do you feel equal to the descent now?'

The going down was even worse. Virginia's high heels made it awkward. 'I'd go barefoot if it wasn't for the thistles.'

'Let's keep to this fence. It looks easier.'

It was not. They came to a stream. The shadows were eerie and deep and the stream was stagnant and blocked. Nicholas peered across it. 'It's pretty narrow. Maybe we can jump it. I'll go first – then I can catch you.'

He leapt and landed in deep black slime. He sank to his knees, made a despairing clutch at anything and nothing, and brought his wrist down on an old partly-submerged jagged drum. He pitched forward with his face neatly in a patch of stinging nettles and was so aware of the need for silence that he swore thoroughly in an intense whisper.

Virginia was so alarmed about it, she jerked her skirt up to give her more width, leapt wildly but better, and landed past him.

'Are you all right, Nicholas?'

'Considering I've only pushed my face through a clump of stinging nettles, torn my right wrist to the bone, dislocated my shoulder and lost my shoe, I can't complain.'

Virginia crept on her hands and knees to the edge of the bog and thrust her hands in. 'Here it is,' she said triumphantly, holding it up. 'It will be better than nothing.'

Nicholas looked things unlawful to be uttered, poured out the worst, and put it on. 'Not far now,' and he took her arm.

Virginia gave a sob of relief when they reached the car. Nicholas released the brake, and between them they got it to the drive entrance. Then they were able to get in and let it coast down the hill towards the main road. 'By that time, we'll be too far away for them to hear the engine.'

When they were a couple of miles on their way back, Nicholas drew in to the side of the road. 'I'll have to get you to tie this wrist up. It's making me feel a bit – groggy.'

Virginia switched on the inside light and whistled when she saw the cut. She brought two handkerchiefs out of her handbag and folded them on the filthy wound, then got Nicholas to press it hard. She hunted through his pockets for a handkerchief, but somewhere in the night's wild doings he had lost it.

'I've always meant to have a first-aid kit and never got round to it.'

'Only one thing for it,' said Virginia, and got out and slipped off her half-petticoat. With great difficulty she tore strips off. 'Something to be said for the days when women wore calico petticoats,' she said savagely. 'This darned thing is dacron and as tough as blazes, and to make it worse, cut on the cross to give that svelte line I'm always advertising. The old ones would have been ideal for chasing incendiarists in. They were three times as wide, and twice as easy to rip.'

Nicholas chuckled, but feebly. Virginia looked at him sharply. She shot out of her door, round the car, opened his door and said: 'Move to my seat – pronto. There's room to put your head down.'

Nicholas obediently moved and put this head between his knees. Finally he lifted it. 'Okay now. But you'll have to drive.'

Virginia got the bandage on and wasted no time on the road. Soon they noticed a small store. 'Whatever will the storekeeper think? We must look wrecks!'

Nicholas knocked at a side-door. Presently a voice demanded aggressively, 'What do you want at this hour? I don't sell petrol.'

'We want to use the phone. We've been chasing burglars. In fact we think we've caught the incendiarists. We want to ring the police.'

A powerful outside light was switched on, there was the sound of a key being turned and bolts drawn. The storekeeper gazed at them searchingly, and Virginia's heart missed a beat when she saw he was carrying a rifle. Then she realized storekeepers in lonely localities run the risk of hold-ups.

'Come in,' he said, 'and we'll hear your tale.'

Nicholas said, 'I'll ring the police first. These beggars have holed up, and we don't think they know they were followed, but it's some distance for the police to come and my early instructions to them were anything but adequate.'

The storekeeper's wife appeared, also in a dressing-gown, and was wide-eyed as she listened. She opened the dampers of the kitchen range and poked some more wood in to the dying fire. She went into the scullery and brought in a baby bath full of hot soapy water. 'We can't have you catching cold into the bargain after chasing burglars into dark valleys and all . . . now, both of you get your feet into this. I'll put some mustard in.'

Virginia thought nothing had ever felt so good on her icy scratched feet. Mr. McIntyre dried them for her on a towel warm from the cylinder cupboard.

Nicholas said, as he waggled his feet about, 'The police aren't too far away. There were no less than three trucks on the roads nearer Cashmere – naturally they were still cruising about. They were the incendiarists all right, they told me. They'd put a match to some petrol-soaked waste before they got out – but the alarm, of course, was given so soon there won't be much damage apart from water.'

Mr. McIntyre bore Nicholas off in search of dry, un-damaged clothes, and when he came back he started to chuckle. Mrs. McIntyre had said to Virginia: 'Now, I'm putting on these woollen stockings that belonged to Granny. I know they aren't exactly glamorous, but there's just nothing like wool for putting warmth into you.' They were a hideous ginger shade, but felt the acme of comfort.

Virginia was past caring. She was wearing huge carpet slippers lined with lambswool, and looked, as Nicholas said, exactly like Minnie Mouse. Nicholas was garbed in heavy working trousers far too short and too wide and ribbed working socks and slipper-boots.

Mrs. McIntyre appeared to be enjoying herself immensely. She produced hot tomato soup out of a tin, fingers of toast, and boiling coffee in no time. Then when Nicholas set his cup down and sighed with repletion, she brought lint and disinfectant.

'We'll have a look at that wrist of yours. Your young lady is worried for fear of infection.'

Virginia could have taken hysterics as she watched the woman unwinding yards of pale green dacron petticoat, edged with nylon frills and dotted with rosebuds, but not when the gash came into full view. Mrs. McIntyre pursed her lips. 'That'll need stitching.'

Nicholas nodded. 'I'll have it done when we get back to town.'

She nodded meaningly at her husband and he went out to the telephone. 'I've rung our doctor,' he said, when he came in, 'he's no distance away and he'd love to be in on this spot of excitement.'

Virginia went off to ring Gwyneth, who by now would be off her head with worry at their non-return. She was. She implored them to get home as soon as they could, but Virginia told her it would certainly take time.

When she returned to the kitchen the doctor was deftly inserting the first stitch. Nicholas was immunized against tetanus, fortunately, but he gave him a penicillin injection and told him it would have to be repeated the next two days.

There was a screech of brakes outside ... the police. In they piled, and the kitchen seemed just full of uniforms. In less than five minutes Virginia glimpsed two men in plain clothes. Good heavens, Murphy and Peter!

'Good life!' she said. 'You two here!'

Peter surveyed her sadly. 'Just imagine us having the nerve to take you out last night in search of copy. If only *we'd* asked if we could tag along by *you*!'

He sighed. 'However, we'll be in at the kill – I hope. They're holding up a stop-press on the last edition. Oh, boy, what a scoop! We'd called in at the station to see if anything had cropped up, and found everything in a flurry of excitement.'

He began to fiddle with his camera. 'Do sit a little nearer Nicholas, Virginia ... contrive to look all excited, even a little loving ... the general public love a bit of romance, you know, especially sandwiched in a crime report. Human interest and contrast.'

'Take your photos when we've got the gang,' said the detective-sergeant, shoving Peter away with his shoulder. 'And don't butt in when I'm still getting information.'

Peter clicked his shutter with all speed, managing to include the sergeant too. Murphy was getting all he could from Mr. and Mrs. McIntyre. To Virginia's life-long regret she wasn't allowed to go along too. 'No,' said the sergeant firmly, 'no women. Mr. Muir will come with us to show us the way, of course – and doctor, you'd better come too, just in case – I suppose we've got to put up with these two newshounds trailing us,' and he gave a would-be savage glare at Murphy and Peter, who appeared quite unmoved.

His aside to the doctor had done nothing for Virginia. She was as tense as a drumskin till they got back – which was within the hour and with the news that three very surprised incendiarists – one had been waiting in the truck outside Fenton's – were now on their way to Christchurch police station.

A young policeman was detailed to drive Nicholas's

151

car back to town – Nicholas felt Virginia had had about enough by now – and even when back in the city, they still had another hour at the station making statements. They began to feel almost heroes and to rather enjoy the fuss made of them.

They drove past Fenton's, found firemen still on duty, and learned that fire damage, as they had thought, was slight, but some of the reserve stocks were saturated. 'Good for business, though,' said Nicholas cheerfully. 'Great publicity, and there'll be a fire sale ahead of us.'

By the time they got to Gwyneth's, however, he looked all in and she insisted he stay the night. In fact she had a bed prepared and hotties in it. She even produced a pair of pyjamas she was making for her son. They were finished except for buttons, and she offered safety-pins instead.

Nicholas grinned. 'I had visions of trying to get into Virginia's flimsies – and I've appeared in enough quaint garments tonight, without that!'

They slept till eleven the next morning.

They made the headlines all right. Gwyneth's house was besieged by reporters ... how she had kept them at bay till the other two had had their sleep out, they did not know. There was no doubt about one thing ... the *Banner* had really scored.

The paper realized the value of one of the principal actors in the real-life drama being a journalist, and engaged her to write it up in her own words, giving it more story value than mere news.

'For once,' said Virginia happily to Nicholas, 'I don't need any local colour.' She sighed wistfully. 'But what a wonderful tale it would have made had I only your permission to relate how your technique consisted of making love to me so that the burglars didn't suspect we'd seen them!'

'You just dare,' said Nicholas, darkling. 'You'll just saw we chatted lightly as we made our way through that dark reserve!'

They had a most hectic time. The damaged goods at the shop had all to be taken stock of for themselves and the insurance company, then heavily reduced. The clearing sale was a nightmare, with all the office staff pressed into serving too, and when that was over, Virginia and Nicholas spent long hours at police-station and court when the case came up.

At the old house in the valley, a tremendous amount of stolen goods had been recovered and Nicholas and Virginia had a spate of thank-you letters to deal with, from various firms. Leicester had rung, of course, as soon as he read the news, duly concerned; so had Nancy, and Virginia's parents. They had even let Penny have three minutes. Penny was only envious she had not been there. She was convinced, had she been, that they would have captured the incendiarists themselves with no help from the police.

Down in Dunedin Mrs. Gordon thought for the first time that perhaps after all Leicester might be wise not to marry Virginia. A girl with a capacity for adventure like that might be decidedly unsuitable for the mistress of a manse. Virginia, had she had any sense of the fitness of things, should have stayed behind and waited to see what Nicholas alone, and the police could accomplish. Even Melanie, with her extravagance and general flibbertigibbet-ness, had never got herself involved like this.

Things quietened down. Fenton's took the necessity for repairs as an opportunity to make substantial improvements, authorized by Sarah, Sarah who was still too deliriously happy with Terence in Australia to be more than mildly excited over the affair. Nicholas said to Virginia, in confidence, that Sarah was very thrilled with Terence's business in Perth and was considering selling this one. 'I'm going into it thoroughly, and if I can raise the money, I'd like to take over the business myself. But not a word to anyone – it unsettles the staff.'

He had a new conference room built, where the heads of departments could meet in more comfort once a month for discussion and decided the old, inadequate one could be used for storing old order books and stationery stocks from the costing department.

Virginia was helping in the move. She'd worked full-time at the shop since the fire, telling herself that it was only decent to help out in emergencies, and shut her mind to the knowledge that it was because she wanted to be near Nicholas.

Alison Marshall was organizing the move. Quite definitely she was a very efficient girl. She had all the shelves numbered and the books sorted before being taken up. There was a tiny room off the bigger one where some very ancient records were to be housed. When Virginia and Alison had gone down for the last lot, Nicholas had gone into the tiny room to see how the work was proceeding. They had no idea he was there. He heard them come in and Virginia say: 'Do you want these taken into the wee room yet, Alison?'

'No, I think we'll sort them out first, Virginia. The table in there is so cluttered up already. Having done all that work downstairs on the sorting, I'd hate them to get mixed up now. These are very old order books.'

Virginia opened one. 'These are signed M.E. Jones. Was Marion Jones in the invoice department once the costing clerk?'

'Goodness, no. This Miss Jones – Margaret Jones – was very different from Marion. Marion is a lovely girl. Margaret was pretty – *if* you admire fluffy types, that is – and a born flirt. She really played with fire, and had never learned her lesson, either. And no better than she ought to be. Quite brazen about it too. I knew she'd only end up one way.'

Virginia sighed. She supposed Alison meant that the girl had made a hasty marriage. Really, the girl had a mind like a cesspool!

Virginia said hurriedly, 'Look, can't I be doing something else while you check these?' trying to change the subject.

Alison said, 'No, there's nothing you can do at the

moment. I've learned the hard way that if you want a thing doing well, you've got to do it yourself.'

'Thanks,' said Virginia drily. 'Go ahead, then.'

Alison hesitated, but only for a moment. She just couldn't resist trying to hurt Virginia, who had succeeded with Nicholas Muir where she herself had failed.

'Of course it served Margaret right. She didn't get Mr. Muir in the end. She met some other poor boob who took her – *and* the baby.'

Virginia froze. She took a firm grip of herself and decided to ignore it. 'Look, I'm quite sure I can do something over here,' and she walked across to some shelves and started dusting the books.

But Alison had determined to say her piece in this golden opportunity of having Virginia to herself. She continued: 'She must have been mad to have thought Mr. Muir would marry her – if he hadn't at the time – they'd worked together at another shop. I think that was why she'd kept the child – as a weapon. It was quite plain to me. She came here at a wage much in advance of the award wage – and had a very comfortable flat and a woman to look after the little girl in her own home during business hours.'

There was a loud bang as Virginia slapped a pile of inoffensive order books on the table in front of Alison, making her jump.

'You can stop talking like that about Nicholas Muir at once! If he were under an obligation to any girl to marry her, he would. He would never let any woman or a child suffer, and you know it! You've just got it in for him, that's all. I can read you like a book. A malicious, lying book! I've known him for months now and have gone out with him, and my father and mother think the world of him, and they're the best judges of character that I've ever known!

'He's incapable of a mean or a traitorous action. You know as well as I do that he's helped many of the girls financially. In fact I've a shrewd idea that because he knows you have an invalid mother, he got Mrs. Fenton to give

155

you substantial rises! And this is how you repay him. *And* it's nothing but sour grapes. If Nicholas gave that girl a much higher wage, it was with Mrs. Fenton's approval, it would have to be. And *she* was no fool. If he worked with her before, he probably knew her story and admired a girl who wanted to keep her baby – even if sometimes it's better to have it adopted. And you've tried to use his kindness to do him an injury.' Virginia stopped, then said, with sheer rage: 'Ohhhhhh! I could respect a girl off the streets more than I could you, you slimy creature! At least they're honest. They don't pretend to be moral. Miss Marshall, I just can't help you any more today. Not till I get over this, anyway. You just make me sick!'

Miss Marshall stood by the table, her knees knocking. If Virginia met Nicholas Muir when she was enraged like this, she'd blurt out the whole thing!

She heard a slight noise behind her and turned to see Nicholas Muir strolling nonchalantly into the room. She was frozen.

He sat himself on the edge of the table and swung one leg carelessly. He looked at Miss Marshall.

'They say eavesdroppers never hear any good of themselves. It seems to be true, doesn't it? Though I heard both, bad and good.'

'Er—' said Miss Marshall.

Nicholas kept on looking at her, waiting for her to say something. But what could she say?

She swallowed. 'I – er – I – that is—'

'There's nothing to say, is there?' asked Nicholas gently. Not for anything would he have explained a word about the situation to this despicable creature in front of him. Besides, Virginia had done it for him, and faith despite lack of knowledge was very sweet at that moment. This girl had an ugly, warped soul.

'I think you would be very wise to plead a headache and go home for the rest of the day. I won't be dramatic and give you notice, but I shall expect you to find another position within a month. I'm quite adamant about that. And

156

if I find you are – out of sheer malice – spreading stories like this about me, anywhere, not only in this shop, I shall take legal proceedings. The only reason I'm not giving you a moment's notice is because I know your mother is dependent upon you, and it would upset her horribly if she had to know why you were sacked. If you're wise, you'll profit by this experience and try to meet life with a cleaner mind. Good morning, Miss Marshall.'

Dumbly, almost thankfully, Alison Marshall left the room.

Nicholas was most relieved when he went downstairs to find Virginia had gone over to the *Banner* with the advertisements. He guessed she'd walk it off before she came back to the shop.

He came down to the flat for dinner that night. When Gwyneth had gone back to her studio (she had shared their dinner) and they had washed the dishes and the two of them were settled in front of Virginia's fire while the winter storm raged outside, Nicholas quite expected Virginia to tell him of the conversation she had no idea he had overheard.

As the night wore on he realized that having spoken her mind to Miss Marshall, she had dismissed the whole thing as unworthy and would not embarrass him by mentioning it. Because she knew a man had a little or no defence against that sort of accusation.

He gazed at her reflectively. She was whipping lace on to the second of the nightgowns she had promised Penny, and in deference to Penny's persisting femininity slant, was adding glamour to a warm garment.

He put his book down. 'Are you still coming with me on that business trip to Dunedin?'

Virginia looked up, amazed. 'Yes, of course. Unless you've gone off the idea of taking me?' This was said with a saucy look.

He laughed. 'You know the answer to that, so I won't pander to your vanity by reassuring you.'

Virginia wrinkled her brow. 'But why did you think I might have changed your mind?'

He couldn't very well say: 'I was wondering if by now doubts of me might have set in,' so he just said, 'Oh, you hadn't said any more about it.'

'No, I've told Mother to expect us both for tea on Saturday. That gives us the week-end at home, then Monday, Tuesday and part of Wednesday for your business calls. We're leaving after lunch on Wednesday, aren't we?'

'Yes. I'd like you to spend most of the time in the sample-rooms with me. I'll take some order books, of course. You can act costing clerk. Give you an insight into that part of the work. Alison Marshall gave me notice today – a month's notice, though she may go before that, I gather. If we don't get anyone before she leaves, you might help out there. How would you like that?'

She didn't look up, appeared to be having difficulty with a knot in her cotton. Then she said. 'I'd rather like it. But you'll probably get someone.'

Nothing more. So she wouldn't even take advantage of that opening.

She folded up her sewing. 'There, that's all ready to take down to Penny. It's got true lovers' knots embroidered on it, little pink bows, and yards of frothy lace. I'll get supper now, Nicky. For some reason or other I feel extraordinarily tired tonight.'

Nicholas thought she had good reason to feel that, but he himself whistled as he drove home.

CHAPTER NINE

VIRGINIA thoroughly enjoyed her week-end. Dad had no weddings on Saturday afternoon, so he and Nicholas had a game of golf at Belleknowes. Virginia took the opportunity to slip round to see Nancy.

Nancy was delighted. The children were at a party and Geoff was at his mother's. They settled down to a cosy chat, then Virginia got down to what she wanted to know.

She said, 'I'm not making any apologies, Nancy. I want to know what went wrong between Leicester and Melanie. I must know.'

Nancy's blue eyes looked troubled. 'Virginia, why do you want to know? Is it because you can't make up your mind to marry Leicester till you know for sure if he's got her out of his system?'

Virginia decided the time had come to be completely frank.

'No. I only want to know for Leicester's sake.'

Nancy bit her lip. 'I don't know what to say. There's been too much interference by other people as it is. Do you mean that if you think he still has any remnant of feeling left for her, you won't marry him, but that you'd try to bring them together again?'

'No. At least – you see, Nancy, I know my own mind now. If Leicester had been my true mate, I wouldn't have let your mother come between us like that. I'd have laughed it off, and realized Leicester and I could make a life of our own. But what your mother said not only put the finishing touch on the doubts I had – doubts as to whether Leicester loved me as I wanted to be loved – but made me examine myself. Was I really in love with him, or was it wishful thinking? Wanting to fall in love, wanting it to be with someone whose existence was so similar to my home setting? And it added up to the fact that both Leicester and I were

159

taking second-best. Then I went to Christchurch and—' she paused, then took the plunge and admitted it '... and I met Nicholas.'

Nancy's eyes held regret that Virginia would never be her sister-in-law, yet joy for a friend that she had fallen in love – truly this time. She said, 'Oh, Virginia! Are you announcing your engagement?'

Virginia held up a hand. 'Nicholas hasn't proposed. But even if he never did it wouldn't matter. I couldn't give any other man second-best.'

Nancy smiled, her eyes misty, 'But it's only a matter of time, I'm sure of that. Poor Leicester! Though—' She stopped.

Virginia said, smiling: 'Go on ... were you going to say that he'll find compensation in England? Well, he will, and maybe he'll find someone before too long. This is what I really came to ask you, Nancy ... is there any chance of him making it up with Melanie? Or is it all over? Because I don't think – with him – it is. There was just something in his voice that convinced me he still loved her when he said her name – a caress, a longing. Did he never try to make it up? What went wrong?'

Nancy got up and walked about the room. 'So many questions! Let me sort them out. Especially as this week I've been milling over the thing until my brain is fagged. But you've helped. Now I know what your feelings are, I think I can – can do something.

'Virginia, Melanie *was* frivolous, even spoilt, but fundamentally sweet. She had no church background, but I always felt that she could develop – given a chance – the chance she didn't get. And Leicester was sweet with her. With her he had a strength of character that revealed his true nature. Leicester needs someone, I think, to depend upon him – a clinging vine. It brings out the best in him.

'Well, all of a sudden she broke it off. It hadn't got as far as an engagement. She said she just knew she couldn't be happy as a minister's wife. It wasn't her sort of life. And off she went – to England, and stayed there.'

Virginia said, hope in her eyes, 'To England? Oh, Nancy, could that be why Leicester is going? – I mean he said he was going if I turned him down.'

Nancy looked unhappy. 'Virginia, this is what's been bothering me this week. No, he certainly wasn't going to be near her. It's just something a lot of young ministers do, as you know, if they're feeling a bit restless – off to do further studies. Look, let me tell you. Melanie and I were very good friends. We wrote to each other for the first year or so, then she stopped writing. You see she had asked me, by letter, if ever Leicester got interested in anyone else, would I tell her. So I told her about you, the fact that you were a minister's daughter and so on, and she said, in answer, that it would probably embarrass me if I felt I had to keep writing.

'Well, suddenly, just this week I got a letter from her. Oh, I should tell you I'd found out later, when Mother let something slip, that it had been she who had induced Melanie to give Leicester up, for his own sake. She'd practically told Melanie that she would ruin his career. Mother made me promise not to tell Leicester. But when I got this letter from her, I went round to Mother. You see, Virginia, the letter was from Christchurch. Melanie's people live there. She's back. She expected to be told that he was married. She asked straight out if he was. I haven't answered it yet.

'Well, I told Mother that I was all but sure you were in love with Nicholas Muir and would marry him. And I asked her to make a sacrifice for Leicester's sake, let me tell him that it was not that Melanie didn't love him enough to take on being a minister's wife, it was because she had been told she wasn't suited to him. Mother has refused that permission. But she got mad with me – and said, unguardedly, that I was to let sleeping dogs lie, that Leicester thought Melanie was married long since and that as soon as you had got over this silly nonsense, you'd marry him.

'I pounced, of course, and she had to admit she had lied to Leicester. I felt sick. I don't like to think Mother was capable of that. But – for Leicester's sake, now that you've convinced me your life belongs to someone else, I'll have to be courageous and do it. I'll write Melanie tonight, tell her that you sensed Leicester still loved her, and that you've found someone else. And I'll ring Leicester.'

Then she sobered up. 'I'd better not ring him till Monday morning. I'll do it after the children go to school. He's got two weddings today, one right now, and one at seven tonight. He detests Saturday night weddings. He likes that to himself to look over his sermon. And I mustn't upset him on a Sunday.'

Virginia agreed with this, knowing how often Mrs. Fergusson had postponed family discussions till the Sabbath was over. 'Yes, that's very wise.' Then a thought struck her. 'Nancy, you still don't know how Melanie feels – for sure, do you? Wouldn't it be ghastly if she's changed, if she no longer wanted to marry Leicester! I mean, these things do happen. Earlier this year, it was all *I* wanted. Wouldn't it be terrible if you told Leicester that, and he bolted up to Christchurch only to find out she didn't want him. I mean when she wrote you, it might have been just to get things tidied up in her own mind. Look, I'm the one who can best convince her that Leicester and I drifted into this. Letters are very difficult. Give me her address, and I'll see her next week as soon as I get back to Christchurch. Thursday, anyway. Then I'll ring you if I think you ought to let your brother know.'

Nancy was vastly relieved. 'I was terrified Leicester might resent me interfering. Oh, Virginia, I do love you.' She put her arms round Virginia. 'And you and I will always be friends.'

It was Wednesday, after an early lunch, and they were saying goodbye to the family. Penny was home with a cold. She kissed Nicholas goodbye, regardless of germs.

'Well, I'll see you in August,' she called, as they left, 'look after yourself, Nicholas.'

As they turned at the corner for a final wave Virginia said, 'What's this about Penny seeing you in August?'

'She's coming up to spend the holidays with you.'

'What? Don't I get consulted? And what can I do with her while I'm at work. I know Gwyneth is home a lot, but I can't impose on her. Besides, you know what Penny is . . . she'd probably take over the studio and fancy herself a genius inside a week.'

Nicholas headed up towards the city, en route to the motorway.

'I've promised her a job in the alteration-room, unpicking seams.'

'My stars! You're certainly looking for trouble.'

Nicholas grinned. 'Penny's the light of my life.'

'You'd better be careful . . . Penny might grow up overnight and marry you out of hand.'

'But, as you once said, my girl, I'm not the marrying sort.'

Inwardly Virginia winced. She didn't want to believe it, but she had to admit Nicholas was the bachelor type. Not that it made any difference to her decision about Leicester. She would make that right. If she couldn't marry Nicholas she would marry no one.

It was a glorious day, one borrowed from summer, but far more precious than any summer day, because you knew it could not last.

Virginia stored up every detail to remember later. The shining evergreen bush; here and there, in swampy places, glimpses of the bright orange beaks of the long-legged *pukeko*, the native swamp-hen, with its blue and black plumage; black and white stilts, diving shags, now and again the opalescent flash as a kingfisher dived like a rainbow-tipped arrow into some wayside stream; the turquoise of the sea that was at full tide at Katiki, creaming back in foaming spray.

They ate their picnic lunch on the shingle banks of the Waitaki River where huge uprooted willows went swirling past because there had been heavy rain in the high country.

'Have you ever been round that detour to Waimate?' asked Nicholas.

'Never. When we go up with Richard or Dad they're such demons for non-stop runs.'

So he took the left turn inland. They were now in South Canterbury, so the hills and dales characteristic of the delightful North Otago country had not yet given place to the flat grazing paddocks and wheat-fields of mid-Canterbury.

'See that little white road up there, curving away up into the hills, doesn't it look inviting?' Virginia said. 'Some day I'll own a car of my own, and then when I see a road that beckons I'll follow it. That road looks as if it's off on secret, delightful business of its own, hiding all manner of quaint pioneer cottages and farmsteadings in the dimples of its hills.'

Nicholas glanced at her, a quirk at the corner of his mouth breaking up his naturally brooding look. She had no idea how like Penny she was at that moment, eyes astar with the delight of imagination. He looked at his watch. 'I dare say our time is our own. I'll take you to explore it now. We'll be doing part of the other half of the journey in the dark anyway. If we find it bears too much to the left, doubling round, we'll have to retrace our steps, but it's ten to one it'll bear to the right again after going so far into the hills. I shouldn't think there'll be even a tiny township tucked away in there. I'm all for it.'

'And I've got a very good sense of direction,' said Virginia smugly.

It was a gem of a road, just the sort to explore on a winter July day that imagined it was December. It meandered in and out of green valleys, up steep hills and across a small plateau. It took its way past little cottages with late, ungathered apples still hanging in russet circles on leafless trees and each with cascading yellow jessamine clinging to verandahs and trellises.

They forded uncounted creek-beds with shallow trickles of water in them. 'They can't have had the rain this side of the Waitaki,' said Nicholas, 'or these would be running higher. I'm glad you had a yen to follow this road, Virginia.'

The high hills around them shut out the sun which was

westering now behind the Southern Alps although they couldn't see the ranges now they were deep in the foothills. The near heights shut out the view of the distant ones. The road was now bearing definitely to the right and seemed to be circling back, so it shouldn't be long before they came to more level country and would probably join up with the Fairlie-Timaru road.

Nicholas changed gear to get up a steep hill. As they came to the top of it he stopped his car in amazement.

It was no lighter up here, and it ought to have been. There was no sun to be seen, just an ominous, huge and inky cloud blotting out the light. Nicholas looked eastward, hoping for a glimpse of the sea and perhaps a bend in the road towards it. There was a great arm of rugged hills running towards the east and the little road continuing to dip and climb through them, narrowing and deteriorating. There was hardly any shingle on it now, just deep ruts on a clay surface that would be a quagmire in rain.

At that moment a great sheet of lightning split the cloud over the sun. Nicholas got out, gazed anxiously down the steep incline to see if, by any lucky chance, it met a better road further on. It didn't.

He came back. 'I think we're in for a spectacular storm. It will be safer to go back than on.'

'I'm terribly sorry, Nicholas. I wish I'd never seen this road.'

He smiled. 'I'm not. It's been a lovely hour's run. We may race the storm back, be off the hills before it reaches here. That centre is a fair distance off.'

It wasn't. They had gone only a couple of miles when Virginia turned her head to listen above the noise of the engine. 'What's that roar?'

'Hail coming across the hills, I think.'

Then it struck them. Nicholas pulled in to the side of the road. In an appalled silence they watched outsized hailstones thudding off the bonnet and instinctively felt like crouching away from the thunder of the ones on the roof. Virginia clung to Nicholas. 'I usually like storms, but this is terrifying, like watching someone in a blazing, violent, un-reasonable temper.'

'It can't last, not at this intensity.'

He was right. The succeeding silence was almost as nerve-shattering as the noise. There were more blinding flashes of lightning, sheet and forked, and long rolls of thunder and heavy intermittent rain.

In no time at all the road was a miniature river. Virginia didn't know it, but Nicholas kept watch for clay banks slipping, though he'd stopped in a fairly safe spot.

They turned to gaze out of the back window, but the rain was coming down it like a cascade. They could gain only an impression of a seething black cauldron of a sky, lit by intolerable glare each time the lightning flashed. The sky seemed to be pressing down on their heads.

'I've seen these electrical storms in the foothills – but always from a safe distance,' muttered Nicholas. Just as he spoke there was a startling crack from a hundred yards ahead of them and a mighty lombardy poplar, majestic in spite of its leaflessness, fell across the road as the clay bank beneath it dissolved into particles. Nicholas had the car door open in a moment, had run round the other side and yanked Virginia out.

'There are two more up there – nearer ... and if they swung, we might cop it. Run down that bank and I'll reverse the car down.'

It was a tricky business. Virginia's heart was in her mouth half a dozen times as the wheels slipped and skidded on the surface of hail. Nicholas guided it to a spot clear of trees, with very low banks, and chocked the wheels with stones. Then he seized her hand. 'Look!' he pointed down a rutted car-track. There, right out in the open, and on fairly level ground, was an old stone hut.

They pelted down the incline and pushed open the door which gave quite easily, and ran into the shelter. Its atmosphere was dank and chilly, but at least it was a refuge from the fury of the storm. A window, entirely without panes, looked north-west towards the storm-centre. They looked at each other and laughed.

Virginia's hair was plastered to her head and she looked exactly like a wet red setter and rivulets of water were running down her shoulder-blades. 'I must look a sight,' she said.

'You look adorable,' he told her. Very pleasant, even if a lie.

That hailstorm lasted twenty minutes. 'If it had come in spring or autumn it would have ruined the countryside,' said Nicholas, going to the fireplace and picking up a huge stone that had bounced into the hearth. 'I've never seen them such a size.'

'I'll go out and see how the car has fared,' he said a little later.

'Not without me,' said Virginia, 'I'm terrified to be left alone.'

Gingerly they picked their way over the frozen heaps of hail. The car was a white mound. They swept off the piles of solidly packed stones with numbing fingers. Trickles of water were forcing their way into the car.

'That will stop, of course, as soon as we get this cleared off. It was too much at once.' He looked up. 'Oh, here we are again!'

The sky in the north was slashed as if someone had slit the atmosphere with a giant pair of scissors. 'It will be torrential rain in a moment,' he prophesied. 'Look, Virginia, grab what we can to make ourselves comfortable in there for a couple of hours. The road's like glass. And we can't go back the way we came because of that poplar.

'We could only' go the other way, and heaven knows what that road'll be like by now. Better to stay here in the dry than get bogged somewhere.' He seized their two suit-cases. 'We'll pile on extra jerseys if it's cold.' There were a couple of travelling rugs and Virginia grabbed the lunch box and sundry packages.

'Now go easy down this slope or we'll have things complicated by broken limbs,' cautioned Nicholas. Just as they reached the hut the rain started again. 'This is some adventure,' he said, and started to laugh.

The hut had an earthen floor beaten hard, a home-made bunk at one end with an indescribable mattress on it, and there were rough cupboards each side of the hearth and a hurricane lamp standing on a rough board table with the middle plank missing. There was a huge pile of *manuka* scrub and pine-cones heaped at one end.

'Isn't it dark?'

Nicholas looked at his watch. 'Yes, of course it's winter and it's nearly five, believe it or not. If we're going to be able to see each other we'd better get this fire going. There's only a little kerosene in the lamp.' He ripped up an old magazine that was lying on the floor, poked it under the scrub, and in a moment the hut was filled with the friendly flame of firelight. Then a huge gust of smoke billowed out, causing them to cough and retreat.

'I might have known,' said Nicholas, 'bird's-nests, no doubt.' He seized a stick and poked vigorously up the chimney. Down fell a heap of last year's nesting and was instantly consumed.

'I think,' said Virginia ruefully, 'we're going to feel very hungry before we get out of here.' She was ruefully examining the contents of the picnic set, two depressed-looking salmon sandwiches, a tomato that had got squashed, and a custard tart in the same condition.

'You wait.' Nicholas opened his suitcase and drew out a large paper-wrapped box. He solemnly undid it, kneeling on the filthy floor, and brought to view a cake unevenly covered with hundreds and thousands, bearing an inscription in pink icing. 'Many happies from Penny.'

'She made it herself and wouldn't show it to you in case you laughed. And *you've* never even asked when my birthday was!'

'Well, when is it?'

'Tomorrow.'

Virginia looked thoughtfully at the cake. 'Dear little Penny! She adores you.' Then she added: 'And if we have to have that for tea, supper and breakfast, we'll be dead with indigestion.'

Nicholas looked quickly at her. 'Then you realize we haven't a hope of getting out of here till tomorrow when the hail has melted?'

'Yes, of course, that's obvious.'

He was vastly cheered to find she was taking it sensibly. He said so.

Virginia looked surprised. 'Well, this is one time when no one will worry over our late arrival. I told Gwyneth we wouldn't be back till Thursday, because I knew she'd worry if we were very late, and Mum and Dad will think we kept to the coast road and would be almost home before this broke anyway.'

That hadn't been what Nicholas had meant, but he let it go. No need to embarrass her.

She shivered suddenly. 'When I think we might have been crushed under that poplar, a bit of discomfort is nothing.'

Nicholas picked up a big iron kettle, gazed doubtfully inside, said well, at least the water would be boiled and that he'd heard water pouring from a spouting, so he'd fill this there. 'I hope we've got some instant coffee left.'

She nodded. 'And some milk, but not much.'

When he got back inside, she was examining the contents of the cupboards and very gleeful. 'I will hand it to you, you know exactly where to get bushed.' She held up a tin of baked beans and one of Irish Stew. 'There's even one of those tins of coffee-and-milk, and some terrible-looking dripping.'

'This will be a shepherd's hut, never built as a home, but still used in the lambing season. They'll often get late snowfalls here.'

They had a good meal, thankful for the plates and cutlery in the picnic set when they saw the two filthy enamel plates and mugs and forks in the cupboard.

They sat on the two fruit cases and Virginia spread the picnic cloth on the indescribable table. The cake was quite good. They began to feel warm at last. They had each had changes of footwear in their cases and their soaked ones were steaming by the fire.

The firelight made the little hut seem cosy and did not reveal too much of the cobwebs and filth. They washed the dishes and set them out neatly for the morning. Nicholas rooted round and found an old large sack. 'I'm going to try to stretch this over those nails at the window-corners to see if we can keep out most of the draught. It may have been used for that before.'

He stood on the box so long looking at a corner of the window, Virginia asked what was wrong. 'A kind of spider I've never seen before.'

'Well, leave it where it is, for goodness' sake! This is no time for bug-hunting!'

Nicholas got the sack up quite tautly and it made a wonderful difference. He blocked up the crack under the door and Virginia picked up a piece of the feathery *manuka* and began to sweep the hearth with it. She fetched a couple of dry sacks from a pile at the end of the bunk and spread them in front for a hearth-rug. Nicholas watched approvingly. 'Cave-woman instincts coming to the fore!' He went over and examined the two chaff bags and the ancient mattress that formed the bedding.

'The mattress is damp, but the bags filled with chaff are not. They'll be more comfy for sitting on than those boxes, especially for an all-night sitting. I hope, though I'm not confident, that these are free from fleas.'

'Nicholas!' wailed Virginia. 'I itch at the thought. How could you?'

He arranged the two boxes for a back, then brought out a bale of hay from under the bunk, twisted off the wire and scattered it over, putting a rug on top. 'Almost luxury. Though I reckon it will be hard by morning.' He tucked the other rug round them to insulate them from the draughts that whistled round the sack as gusts swept against the hut, and they settled down with a pile of dusty magazines they had found in the cupboard. There were some ancient *Humours*, some ditto *Digests*, and a couple of lurid magazines that Nicholas hastily tucked under the hay. Virginia did notice, but had the sense not to ask to see them.

Suddenly there was a scuffling at the window. Virginia clutched Nicholas. The sack flew off the nail at a lower corner and in scrambled a small black cat. 'Another pilgrim of the storm,' said Nicholas. 'Come right in, puss.'

It gave them a baleful emerald glare and darted under the bunk. Virginia roused up. 'I'll give it the last of that milk.'

Nicholas groaned. 'I thought that would be nice for our coffee in the morning.'

She said, 'Well, there's that coffee-and-milk in the tin.'

'Yes, but that's made with sweetened milk and we both hate it . . . oh, all right, give it to it.'

It was some time before the cat ventured out to lap it. When it was done it seemed a little less suspicious. It let Virginia stroke it. She said, 'I think it's been a household pet, but gone wild. Poor thing, it's soaking.' Suddenly it twisted round and emitted a weird howl. Virginia backed hastily. 'Whatever is the matter with it?' The cat repeated the performance.

Nicholas started to laugh. 'Don't you know? In a very little while we're going to have more pilgrims.'

'You mean she's going to have kittens?'

He nodded. In the next ten minutes there were two tiny mites there, as black and wet as their mother, and the cat was purring and licking them in an ecstasy of maternal joy. Virginia tried to tempt her then with the Irish Stew they were saving for breakfast, but she would have none of it.

'Better leave her alone, Virginia. I don't think she's finished yet.'

'But would she be purring if she was still going to have more?' asked Virginia, who had had no experience at all of feline maternity.

'Yes. She'll have a brief spell without pains.'

The cat began howling again and Nicholas laid his magazine down and came over. He soothed her with a gentle hand. 'She's not much more than a kitten herself. Her first litter, I'll be bound. Oh, I see what's wrong. This one is coming the wrong way. I'll have to help things along. You stroke her head, and speak soothingly. But don't touch her kits.'

In two minutes the last kitten was lying beside the others, more dead than alive. Nicholas said: 'Took too long ... another moment or two and it would have suffocated. I've probably bruised its two back legs a bit – it's much easier with a bigger animal – but it may recover.' He began massaging the kitten. Presently there was movement, and the cat took over, giving Nicholas's hand a rough swipe with her tongue in gratitude.

Nicholas was as unperturbed as if he had been handling an order in the shop. Virginia was amazed. He scooped up some paper, mopped up, then burnt it. 'Thank goodness there's some hot water in that kettle. Oh dear, there's only that pan big enough to wash my hands in. I know. Virginia, pour some into the sandwich container, would you? And get the soap out of your sponge-bag.'

He grinned at her. 'You're looking at me with admiration and awe. Keep it up, I can take a lot of that. I used to spend all my holidays on a farm at Weston when I was a kid. Many's the lamb or calf I've helped bring into the world.'

Virginia thought dazedly that she was constantly discovering new facets of Nicholas's character. And she liked them all.

'But I've never played midwife to a cat before. It takes you to drag me into amazing adventures – rescuing you from men you don't want to be rescued from, chasing burglars, and now spending the night in a primitive hut!'

'Well, I like that! You can't possibly hold me responsible for the burglars. If it hadn't been for your pipe—'

He broke into this with: 'Gosh, this is all mod cons with a vengeance! I didn't know you had a hottie with you. Good idea, it will keep our feet warm if the fire dies down.'

'Oh, it's not for us. I'm going to tuck it under the sack you put the cat on. Then that poor little weak kitten will get a bit of extra warmth.'

Nicholas gave way to mirth. 'Anyway,' he said, when he sobered up, 'I'm going to put it to its mother in a moment. Once they get a drink, they perk up in great style.'

The cat made no demur when Virginia lifted them all nearer the fire. 'Absolute domesticity,' said Nicholas.

Before long he said, 'I think if I put this log on, I'll have to make that the last. There's just about enough wood left to cook breakfast.'

Virginia shifted her position and stifled a yawn. 'We're going to have terrible cricks in our necks tomorrow morning,' she said. 'I thought we'd stay awake all night, that we'd be cold and uncomfortable, but—' she stifled another yawn— 'I'm so darned sleepy I don't think I can keep awake much longer.'

In another moment she was asleep against his shoulder, her hand in his, her head under his chin. Nicholas looked down on her. Her trust in him was the expression of her disbelief in the slander Miss Marshall had tried to put across.

He looked his fill ... at the tousled red hair, the dark fan of the tawny lashes against her cheek, the rise and fall of her breast. This was what happened in all the best novels, he thought, only usually the hero played his (Nicholas's) part. Well, he was glad he had shared this, not Leicester Gordon.

He felt confoundedly sleepy. In the novels the hero always stayed awake, guarding his lady's rest. Perhaps he was no knight. And perhaps there were more perils in those days. No doubt the knights of old were made of tougher fibre or – not half so in need of sleep. Nicholas's head fell against the copper hair.

The campers woke stiff and cold in the grey dawn, but the wind and rain had ceased. The cat had eaten the stew during the night and was overwhelmingly smug in her maternal pride this morning.

'Anyone'd think,' Nicholas told her severely, 'you'd done

it all yourself!'

By the time they had boiled the kettle and heated the amount of stew Virginia had left them, and topped off their breakfast with fruit cake with gooey icing, the sun was making a golden glory of the outside world.

They stood in the doorway, watching it with delight. The light had caught every drop of rain pearled on every glass-blade, till the whole hillside was glinting crystal and silver.

Over to the west the ranges, which now were mantled with dazzling white, caught the reflection of the sunrise in the east and glowed in all the colours of a prism, rose, amethyst, mother-of-pearl.

'It's been well worth last night's storm to see a sunrise like this, Nicholas,' Virginia said softly.

She glanced up at him, looking much less debonair than usual.

She said, 'Happy birthday, Nicholas,' and reached up and kissed him. 'Thank you,' he said, and made no attempt to kiss her back.

They tidied up the hut, carefully raked out the ashes, brought in piles of wet wood from the edge of the bush, knowing it would soon dry inside. 'We'll stop at the first house we come to, find out who owns this hut, and leave some cash to replace what we ate – and get them to ring the A.A. about that fallen tree. Virginia, what on earth are you doing with my scarf?'

She was arranging it carefully in an old carton she had found. 'I'll buy you another. I want to put the cat and kittens in this to put in the car.'

'Look, it's well able to take care of itself, with all this forest about. It's – oh, all right, you can stop looking at me like that. I can't refuse you anything when you do. I might have known that you'd insist on taking it home.'

The car took some starting, and the going was far from easy, but they pulled up at the first house. It was quite near the road for a New Zealand farmhouse. Nicholas said hastily: 'Just stay in the car with the kits.' It would save embarrassment.

He was back before long. 'This is the worst bit of the road, but a couple of miles further on it improves and then it isn't more than ten miles to the main road into Timaru. Worst storm in the district for twenty-five years. Their phone is out, wires down everywhere. They said we were welcome to the shelter.'

Virginia said: 'So we'll have to ring the A.A. from further into town. Nicholas, tell me what you said? Did you say you and your wife had to take shelter?'

He grinned. 'No, I said, "I and my companion." Satisfied?'

'Yes.' She laughed. 'Poor Mrs. Gordon, if she knew about this, she'd think Leicester was – Leicester should drop all idea of me as a wife.'

Nicholas didn't think there was much chance of Mrs. Gordon hearing about it, but he did wonder how Leicester would take it. That was supposing Virginia told him. And it would be foolish not to, because it would make any chap wonder, if it wasn't mentioned and then found out. It would make something clandestine out of what had been an unavoidable adventure, treated sanely so far. It had been lightheartedly and sweetly shared.

When they arrived at the house by the Avon, they found Leicester installed in Virginia's sitting-room. 'I didn't know you were away, Virginia, till Gwyneth told me. You've both been to Dunedin?' He glanced quickly from Virginia to Nicholas and back again.

Nicholas looked at Virginia. For some reason she had gone white. He said, very quickly, 'It was a business trip, Leicester. Virginia played costing clerk and came round the sample-rooms with me. It gave her an opportunity of a few days at home at the same time.'

Virginia said, and Nicholas could see a pulse beating quickly in her throat, 'Do you happen to have heard from Nan? I mean she – I mean did she ring you Monday after all?'

Leicester said, surprised, 'No, should she have?'

Virginia's speech was always so direct her fumbling caused both of them to gaze at her. 'Well, yes. At least at one stage she was going to. Then she decided she wouldn't. But I thought — I mean rushing up to Christchurch like this, that—' she stopped.

Leicester blinked. 'I didn't rush. I stayed with a friend in South Canterbury who was in college with me, Monday and Tuesday nights. He has a manse there. And then I went up to Fairlie and spent last night there. I'm having a few days off.'

Virginia recovered herself. So he didn't know yet about Melanie. She so very much wanted to see Melanie herself first. Because if Leicester cared for Melanie as she herself cared for Nicholas, it would be dreadful to raise his hopes if Melanie did not want to take things up again.

Before she could think of anything to say, Nicholas struck in. 'Then if you were at Fairlie, you'd experience that freak storm?'

'Did we what? Never saw anything like it. Trees and power-lines down all over, slips in Burke's Pass, flash floods — some motorists were stranded. A party of girls spent the entire night on top of their car.'

'We were stranded too, but we struck it luckier than they did. Virginia had never been round by Waimate, so we went through there and she spotted a lovely little road that lured us on. That storm caught us with about five minutes' warning — that hail! And a huge poplar fell in front of us when we turned back because the road was deteriorating. And of course once that road got two inches of hail on it, freezing solidly, it was impassable. But we didn't dare stay in the car, there were too many trees bordering the road. We found the filthiest hut you could imagine, but out in the open. And it had a bit of food in it. A shepherd's hut, and firewood. But oh, boy, what an uncomfortable night! There were two boxes, a couple of bags of chaff and a bale of hay, on a dirt floor. We ache in every limb.'

Leicester took it all without raising an eyebrow. Of

course in the circles Virginia and Leicester moved in, there was no room for sly jests or cheap gibes. And he knew Virginia.

'Jolly lucky you found a place like that. And that the tree missed you.'

Virginia thought of something. 'And what do you think, Leicester, a cat sought shelter from the storm too, and she had three kittens. I'll show you.' And she darted out to the car.

Leicester raised a comical eyebrow. 'You don't mean to tell me, Muir, that Virginia insisted on bringing that cat and kittens all the way here?'

'I do. She couldn't be convinced that cat wouldn't starve. And she thought she needed lashings of milk herself to help her support three kits. Really, what a night!'

The two men gave way to mirth. It took Virginia some time to get the box out of from where she had wedged it so that the cat wouldn't spring out every time they opened the door.

It gave Leicester time to say: 'I say, Muir, I'd like Virginia to myself tonight. I've something to discuss with her, and you've had a pretty fair run. I'd like a fair go.'

'Right.' Nicholas showed no resentment. This pleasant dalliance had to come to an end some time. It was quite evident that Leicester wanted a straight answer this time.

Nicholas excused himself on the grounds that he must call in at the shop and see what the takings had been in his absence, as he had to get the weekly report off to Sarah.

'I'll come out to the car with you and get the rest of my gear,' said Virginia, and she seemed oddly preoccupied. Perhaps she had already guessed what Leicester was here for. Well, it was probable that Leicester now valued her more than he had once.

At the car Nicholas stopped and looked down on her.

'Virginia?'

'Yes?'

'Leicester wants to have you to himself tonight. He's come up to discuss something with you. You can guess what.

I think he's determined on a straight answer this time. You've fobbed him off before and I think it's had the desired effect. He'll probably never take you for granted again. I just hope not.

'I – I think our spot of delightful foolery has served its purpose. You're not now just the girl his mother thought so suitable. He's had to pursue you. I think this is where we ring the curtain down on our pleasant dalliance. By the way, never reveal your technique, and certainly never call it that – it has a Charles the Second smack about it.'

Virginia nodded. She hadn't raised her eyes and she was standing very still. 'Yes, I suppose so. Yes, I agree with everything you say, Nicholas. And thank you for being so – kind.'

'It was very easy to be – kind,' he said, and neither said any more for a queer, breathless few moments.

Then Nicholas said: 'I – I didn't expect it to finish up so soon. You've been – a grand little pal. I've never had just this quality of comradeship from a girl before. Any – any chance of having a farewell outing? I don't think Leicester should grudge me that. He'll look upon me as the unlucky loser, you know!'

Virginia nodded because she was sure her voice wouldn't sound normal yet. *He's very, very sure I'm saying yes to Leicester.*

'Would it be asking too much?' persisted Nicholas, not seeing the nod because he was staring at a log floating down the river.

'No, I don't think it would be asking too much. I'm sure Leicester will be going back late tomorrow. His week-end is looming up. I owe you – a – a lot. Let's make it tomorrow night.'

'Thank you, Virginia. Go back to your old hours – come in just before twelve. You must be tired – what with last night, and now this, except that what Leicester has to say to you may act like a shot in the arm.'

Virginia smiled faintly. He drove away.

She didn't go back in to Leicester right away. She went

across to the river-bank and leaned on the wooden railing looking at an upside-down world reflected there.

She watched it for quite some time. She felt numb. Yes, it was a topsy-turvy world, especially hers. It seems this was where her revolt ended and the pleasant dalliance with it.

Oh, well, you couldn't play round on the fringe of things for ever. But it had been fun while it lasted. She knew exactly what she was going to do. Nicholas would think she had accepted Leicester. In a week or two she would say she was going back to Dunedin because it was nearer Leicester's parish and she would see him more often. And she would slip out of Nicholas's life, Nicholas who hadn't wanted any more than the comradeship they had enjoyed, plus a little light flirtation when the mood took him.

She supposed that even when she was quite old, she would take out the memory of it all, and look it over and be glad for it.

She went back into the room and as Leicester came across to her she held up her hand. 'Leicester, Nicholas told me that you had something to discuss. Well, I realize what it is and I know we can't fiddle around any longer. But it so happens I've got something terribly urgent to attend to. I'm going to ring for a taxi now and get it over. I don't know when I'll be back, but I've just got to see to it. Look, will you get those kittens nicely settled and get something from Gwyneth for the mother?'

Leicester couldn't help it, he laughed. 'It's just like you to mix up drama with animal care! But let's get them settled and I'll run you wherever you want to go to, and wait for you, no matter how long it takes.'

But she was adamant. Inwardly she was thinking: Imagine asking him to drive to Melanie's old address! And she may not be in, I may have to wait. And I don't know how she'll receive me.

She got her taxi, asked him to drive to Fendalton and was there before she had half her thoughts marshalled.

She stood outside, trying to summon up her courage. If Melanie's mother or father opened the door she would have to give her name. And they might just know it. Oh dear!

The door opened and out came a girl with a pair of scissors. She was slight and not very tall, with smooth fair hair and cornflower blue eyes and the most exquisitely oval face. She gazed at Virginia, hesitating with one hand on the latch of the gate. 'Oh, hullo,' she said, in a voice that was like a chime of bells, and her eyes crinkled into a smile. 'Are you just coming in? Do you want one of us?'

So Virginia had to plunge. 'Are you Melanie?' she asked.

The blue eyes widened. 'Yes, why—'

Virginia gulped noticeably. 'I want to see you, and though you may think it strange, I'd like to see you alone. I – I've got a message for you, from Nan. Nan Gordon that was.'

The colour came up into the rather thin cheeks and in that moment she looked younger and more vulnerable. Melanie said quickly, 'Then come over here into this little summer-house that's the pride of Dad's heart. It's a bit cold, but if you'd rather—'

'It will do beautifully.'

The girl led the way, put the scissors down on a table, and turned to Virginia, her hands clasped in front of her, waiting with all her might and main.

Virginia said, 'Nan had your letter and didn't know what to do. She asked my advice . . . she didn't know if she should answer it first, or ring Leicester first at Greenhaughs. I told her to wait till I'd seen you. I live in Christchurch, but I was in Dunedin for the weekend. You see, what Leicester doesn't know is that you're still single. He's thought for years – well, soon after you got to England – that you were married.'

Melanie's cheeks had paled again, but now they glowed. 'Married – but how could he? Do you mean that was why he never tried to make it up? To reach me again? I always hoped if he – found he couldn't live without me – that he might follow me to England and there we would have had a chance of making a happy marriage – away from his mother – I might even have made a tolerably good minister's wife. But why did he think I was married?'

Virginia said quietly, 'Mrs. Gordon told him you were. And of course, Leicester has never known that it was his mother who got you to give him up. Well, he tried to patch up his life. Egged on by his mother he began keeping company with someone else.'

'Yes, yes, I know,' said Melanie feverishly, 'she's called Virginia Fergusson. I expect you know her.'

Virginia nodded.

Melanie said, 'But I can't break that up. Besides, he might not want me now. This girl is a minister's daughter. Ages ago Nan told me about her. She'll know the ropes. Her father won't own race-horses – though Leicester always liked Dad – but Mrs. Gordon thought it was awful. Worldly. But I couldn't make another girl suffer.'

Virginia said: 'You won't. She realized ages ago that Leicester and she were very tepid about each other. That's an absolute fact, Melanie. She left home to think it out. Marriage is too big a step not to be sure. And she almost immediately met someone else whom she loved dearly. She and Leicester had just drifted, but he and she have remained quite good friends. But she knows that he really loves you. She says that even the way he speaks your name reveals that.'

Melanie was dithering between hope and disbelief. She struck her hands together. 'But how can I be sure of that? *You* seem to be sure, but how about her? And how can you know all this?'

This was the moment. Virginia dimpled. 'Because *I'm* Virginia Fergusson,' she said, and struck an attitude, hand to her heart, 'and I love another!'

Suddenly Melanie's laughter bubbled up and rang out. She seized Virginia's hands, 'Oh, you wonderful, wonderful, courageous girl! I'm sure I'm dreaming. What do I have to do? Where is Leicester, and how do I get to Greenhaughs? I mean he is there, isn't he?'

'He's in Christchurch. In Avonside, at my flat. I've just got back from a trip down to see my people with – this man I told you of. He's the manager of the firm I work for. And Leicester has been at Timaru and Fairlie visiting minister friends and is staying with another in Christchurch tonight. He – dropped in to see me. Melanie, he doesn't even know yet you're here – here and unmarried. Nan and I felt we didn't dare tell him until we found out for sure if you still cared. Will you tell your parents you have to go out? You could ring for a taxi. And you can have my flat all evening. You can cook him a meal if you want to, when you've come up for air.'

Melanie said, 'Here in Christchurch . . . twenty minutes away . . . I can't believe it! It's been thirteen thousand miles distant for so long. No need for a taxi . . . I've got a car. I brought it back with me. Will you come in and meet my parents?'

'No – it would take too long explaining. Any chance of you getting away without them knowing yet? I mean, I want nothing to prevent you meeting him, with all the barriers down, as now.'

'I'll fix it,' Melanie whirled away, her blue frock disappearing down a hydrangea walk.

She was back in five minutes, dangling car keys, and had stopped, evidently, only long enough to renew her make-up and fling on a fleecy pale blue coat that matched her frock.

Virginia said, 'I know you'll hate the delay, but I want you to stop at the first phone booth. I want Leicester to know – before he sees you – that you're not married. Please?'

Melanie felt she owed Virginia so much that she was content to have this left entirely in her hands. This was a miracle, something she still couldn't believe.

Virginia got Gwyneth to call Leicester to the phone.

She said, 'Leicester, I'm going to talk fast and to the point, and you're not to stop me. Not once! Now listen. I'm on the way to you with the most delightful surprise you've had in your life, and I want you to be put

182

in the picture so you can enjoy it to the full . . . no, Leicester, no interruptions. I was wiser than I knew when I ran away to try to know my own heart. I not only met Nicholas but I found out that you'd taken the hardest of knocks before I knew you.

'I don't blame you one scrap for making up your mind that there were other fish in the sea. Many marriages based on just that are very happy. But not for you, and not for me. Now, Leicester, it was all a mistake about Melanie getting married.' She gulped – she mustn't make more trouble – 'I think someone must have told your mother wrong. She's never been even engaged to anyone else. She's here in Christchurch. She wrote to Nan and asked if you were married yet. I'm in this telephone box ringing you, and she's outside in her car and she's on the edge of her seat. I'm bringing her over to you *now*. But I've got only one stipulation to make – she is never, never, never to know that you'd come up to ask me for a final answer. It could only have been "No" because of Nicholas. Now, I'll bring her to the door of the flat – no, the gate – and she'll walk in on you, and the rest is up to you – and let me tell you, this is all due to Nan. You've got a sister in a thousand. And, Leicester, don't be too hard on your mother. She's learned her lesson. So . . . just God bless. Bye-bye.' And she hung up.

They drew up at the house with the tinkling fountain, when the winter evening was just starting to shut in the houses with a friendly darkness.

Virginia unlatched the gate, pushed Melanie through, and saw Leicester waiting for her just inside the door. Virginia thought with a real stab of pain, oh, if only that were Nicholas, waiting for me! Then she pulled her gate shut and went along the street to Gwyneth's gate. She'd have the evening meal with her, because Gwyneth must be warned. She must be warned too, that the two downstairs, whom they would be congratulating later, must not know that she and Nicholas were *not* on the point of being engaged. . . .

CHAPTER TEN

VIRGINIA rang Nicholas at ten the next morning. 'Nicholas, any chance of my having the day off?'

'Sure ... too much excitement? Or is it the matter of planning a celebration?'

'Well, it is that. A small luncheon.'

'Right. But you won't forget you're promised to me tonight ... or has Leicester forbidden it? I don't really blame him if he has.'

'I didn't ask him,' retorted Virginia, beginning to feel a little more normal.

'Deceiving him already?' reproved Nicholas. 'I take it I'm to offer felicitations?'

There was no answer. The line had gone dead. Nicholas dialled Gwyneth's number, but got no reply at all. Virginia must have been ringing from town. Perhaps she and Leicester were making a tour of the jewellers.

It was a busy day at the shop, especially after his few days' absence. It was late shopping night, but for once Nicholas didn't care. He felt that the staff problems, the difficult customers, the locking up could all be left to the accountant. It was nearly six when he stepped into the street lit by countless flashing neon signs and the lights of a myriad cars.

Virginia was reading by her fire. He could see her through the glass door.

'I wasn't sure if you'd come down now, or after you'd had your meal.' She stood up, but did not come across to him.

She was wearing a dress of soft green wool with full bishop sleeves and a plaited leather belt. 'What are we going to do tonight, Nicholas?'

'We'll have tea over at the bay. I promised you long ago

I'd take you there again some day.'

Virginia felt inwardly amused. Evidently since Leicester had not turned a hair over the night they spent together in the storm, Nicholas wasn't worrying about the proprieties any more. She supposed it was a compliment, and he had no idea of the tumultuous feelings she kept in check—

'Nicholas, this is our last evening together. Do we have to talk about Leicester, or could we—? Well, these months have been such glorious fun – riotous really, even if not for lasting – could we just pretend everything is like it used to be . . . carefree and lighthearted?'

'Yes, if that's the way you want it, Virginia.' He looked at her sharply. She looked as if she hadn't slept for a week. There were shadows under her eyes almost like faint blue bruises. He took her face between his fingers for a moment.

'You look as if some fresh air'd do you good. Get your coat,' and he released her suddenly as if he sensed her embarrassment. The thought of Leicester was going to lie between them after all.

'Going to be a frost,' Nicholas said, as they stepped out into the street. The street lamps were pools of gold reflected in the gentle Avon. Above them the Milky Way was a blaze of star-crusted splendour; a pale moon was already climbing above the weeping willows, and the little fountain tinkled its darling tune as they passed by.

Virginia wanted to clutch time to her, to hold it still. But it seemed no time before Nicholas was fitting that enormous key into the lock of the cottage.

As he switched the lights on he said, 'You aren't wearing a ring . . . didn't it fit?'

She shook her head. 'Too large, so it's being made smaller.'

True enough, Melanie hadn't been wearing it when they had met for the luncheon celebration.

Nicholas brought the provisions in from the car. Virginia put a match to the fire set in the old range. She had a queer nostalgic stab for the dirty stone hut of two nights ago. That had been a gay adventure. Farewells were the very dickens. Even if you had known from the start a thing was temporary, it could still be painful to say goodbye.

Because that was what this was, in all truth. The last time she would go out with Nicholas. Later tonight she'd tell him she was going back to Dunedin till the wedding. He'd never know, till much later, that it hadn't been Virginia's wedding. Because if he knew now he might, out of pity, propose. And if she married Nicholas, it would have to be because he loved her as she loved him. Nothing less would satisfy her. She thought she'd go to England soon after she left Christchurch.

She went into Beth's bedroom to take off her coat. She felt in her pockets for a handkerchief and brought out a crumpled piece of paper. She smoothed it out. It was the piece of paper she had scribbled the corsetry ad on at North Beach. On the other side was the poem, word-perfect as it had come to her, that she had refused to let Nicholas see. She read it slowly.

'The loveliest thing in the world tonight?
Was it a moonbeam, silver-white?
Was it a wave that broke in spray
As a white-winged seagull skimmed the bay?
Was it a star, remote and fair
Or the pirate touch of the salt-tanged air?
... No, 'twas the sound of your voice to me
As we trysted there by the ceaseless sea.'

She crumpled the paper between her fingers and went out to the range. She lifted up the stove-lid and dropped it in. No need to keep it. Those words were written on her heart. And it would never do to have Nicholas see them. Tea was going to be a stiff affair and an ordeal she feared. Still, there was always small talk.

When they had finished, neither of them quite meeting the other's eyes all through the meal, Nicholas said: 'Let's walk down to the beach.' They went down slowly through this fragrant garden that hardly knew the touch of winter, here in this sheltered fold of the hills. Daisies still bloomed and overran the paths, brushing against you, and there was heath and rosemary and balm. Balm. Would she ever see it again without remembering? There was holly, and cotoneaster with red berries, and they had already passed the spindle-tree that kept the witches from the door . . . it was a very narrow track that led down to the sea, and it forced them together.

Nicholas had to take her hand to save her from stumbling, but he found her fingers cold and unresponsive.

It came a little easier to talk, down at the shore. They didn't have to avoid locking glances and there were the little waves to watch as they lapped the sand, and the lighthouse down the harbour.

He had hoped they might fill the evening in with banter and a little light lovemaking as they had always done, and he hoped that Virginia might kiss him goodnight very sweetly. It would be something to remember. But even though they had agreed not to talk about Leicester, now she was promised to him, naturally she was withdrawn and remote.

The situation had got well out of hand as far as his own feelings were concerned. He mustn't flatter himself that Virginia had ever regarded him as anything but a fill-in, a spur to Leicester who – fool that he had been – had not loved her as she loved him. But he had to look at it fairly and squarely from Virginia's viewpoint. He was going to play fair. He only wanted her happiness. And if that happiness lay with Leicester, well, he'd certainly served her there, had stirred the laggard lover up.

The wind from the sea blew a strand of Virginia's hair across Nicholas's face and something snapped in him . . . all his knight-errantry, all his unselfishness, his high resolve.

He turned roughly and grabbed her, his fingers biting into her shoulders with the strength he did not know he was exerting.

'Virginia, let's have done with this nonsense! I don't care if you *have* said yes. He'll never love you and cherish you as I will . . . I can't let you go, do you hear? It's all been a mistake. I'm sure I can make you love me more than you've ever loved him. I can't bear it. I can't bear to think of you being taken for granted again ... when there's no more competition. Virginia ... Virginia ...' and he crushed his mouth down on hers.

Virginia felt as if every pulse in her found expression in that kiss. She felt as if the Milky Way reeled above her. Oh, he loved her, he loved her, and he was agonizing over the situation – and she couldn't get her mouth free to tell him it was all right. That she was free ... and his, that she'd been his ever since they had first met ... He suddenly released her, looked down on her and demanded: 'See ... see? You responded. You couldn't help yourself ... Oh, Virginia, Virginia ...!'

She put a hand against his mouth, said, 'Nicholas, Nicholas, listen! *I'm not engaged to Leicester.* The answer was no, always has been ever since I met you . . . only he wouldn't believe it. But he never loved me as he ought. Yesterday I restored him to the only girl he ever loved ... his Melanie ... oh, it's too long a story, and tonight is *ours*, not theirs. Oh, Nicholas, Nicholas, my love, stop wasting time!'

Yet he held her off for a moment, unable to really take it in till he had searched her eyes and made sure. And she waited for that. Then she said, on a half-sob, half-laugh, 'Oh, darling, darling, I thought you weren't a marrying man. I thought it was only pleasant dalliance with you ... and you nearly broke my heart when it seemed you wanted me to marry Leicester.' And then she couldn't say any more for a long, long time.

Gone Nicholas's suavity, gone his man-of-the-world air. He was just a man with a deep hunger. When he released her, she wasn't allowed to speak. He put a finger on her lips. 'Fair go. My turn! Sweetheart, you must be the most priceless idiot – though I admit I tried to hide from you the fact that I was head over heels in love with you – but I felt it must be written all over me. I've loved you – consciously – from the day I swept you out to the car away from Leicester.

I got such a shock at lunch-time. I suddenly realized here was the one woman I wanted to see across my table every day, for the rest of my life.

'It was always bowling me out. I was always biting back the things I wanted to say to you. That first time we came here – and you were so adorably confused and worried about Sarah Fenton. Remember how we went out in the *Sarah Jane*? And then I said to you that it was my mother's name – and your second name? I only just stopped myself from saying: "We'll call our first daughter Jane after the two of you." I was as sure of what I wanted as that. And if you don't think I'm a marrying man, ask your parents. That was the day I came back from seeing them. – Gosh, I thought your mother would die when you said that about me when Penny and I were washing dishes. You see, I'd gone to see them earlier and told your mother and father that I loved you, that I hoped you might marry me, that while you were in Christchurch you would be in my care. They said you must please yourself. But they were very sweet. Your mother said, "She must please herself, but I'll be honest with you, Nicholas. I think you love her as she deserves to be loved. I'm quite sure Leicester doesn't." ' He stopped, 'Come on, don't hold out on me. When did *you* know?'

'I tried to fight it, Nicholas. I thought it was only kindness on your part – the same sort of chivalry that made you try to rescue me the day you thought Leicester was Les. But I knew for real that weekend at Dunedin . . . you went out to walk on the beach and suddenly I couldn't be bothered with the others. I wanted to get after you. And when I climbed up to you on the rocks I realized for once and all that your world was my world.'

That reminded Nicholas of something that had happened that weekend. 'But no wonder I had my doubts, no wonder I thought I might not fill the bill . . . do you realize, Virginia, that you're marrying a draper? Not a professional man, just someone in the rag-trade? A draper, mark you, with two exclamation marks after him! An effeminate creature in an effeminate trade!'

Virginia was gazing at him as if she thought he'd suddenly gone raving mad. 'What are you talking about, Nicholas? Yet I seem to have heard that before.'

'It *should* ring a bell, you brat! You wrote it and I read it that Sunday morning in one of your scrapbooks. It gave me some bad moments.'

They had started to climb back to the house now, hand-in-hand.

Virginia paused on the path. 'But didn't you realize how many years ago I wrote that? When I was an insufferable creature in my teens, with – I realize now – less sense than Penny!' She tugged at his sleeve. 'Besides, Nicholas, I'd marry *you* if you were a dustman!'

'I seriously doubt the truth of that wild statement, but let it go. Besides, what an extremely unromantic thing to be said by a novelist. Juliet said it better, I think.'

'What did she say?' Her face was upturned to his.

He looked down on her and said softly: ' "And all my fortunes at thy feet I'll lay, and follow thee, my lord, throughout the world." '

Virginia's eyes were shining. 'Then it means that ever since Shakespeare's day women have felt as I do – about their men. Nicholas, when shall we be married?'

He laughed. 'Daft creature! *I'm* supposed to be asking *you* that. We'll get married when the cherries are in blossom, and come here for our honeymoon. If you want a cruise I'll take you in January, but I feel a honeymoon is just two people, quite alone. I couldn't stand a hotel. So that, my love, means September. Gives you two months. I can't wait longer.' He laughed again. 'Dare I take liberties with Housman's verse? You know I said it didn't fit the Southern Hemisphere?'

'It's your night, Nicholas. Take what you like.'

He said, ' "Loveliest of trees, the cherry now
Is hung with bloom along the bough" ' . . . and added:
'And stands above the harbour tide
Decked for my September bride!'

190

He caught the shine of tears in her eyes, bent and brushed his lips over hers. 'Tears of happiness? I don't mind that kind. I say, what kind of a witch are you? You've made a poet out of me.'

Virginia said, 'Stay that way, Nicholas, I like it.' She turned and swept the hillside with happy eyes . . . the golden lights of snug homes across the bays, the netted cherry trees on the next hill looking like an acre of silver cobwebs in the moonlight, then looked up to where their own lighted home beamed out a welcome to them.

'Let's go inside, Nicky,' she said.

Have You Missed Any of These Best Selling

HARLEQUIN ROMANCES?